2

THE DAYSTAR VOYAGES

WIZARDS OF THE GALAXY

GILBERT MORRIS
AND DAN MEEKS

MOODY PRESS
CHICAGO

Moody Press, a ministry of the Moody Bible Institute,
is designed for education, evangelization, and edification.
If we may assist you in knowing more about Christ
and the Christian life, please write us without obligation:
Moody Press, c/o MLM, Chicago, Illinois 60610.

All Scripture quotations, unless indicated, are taken from the *New
American Standard Bible,* © 1960, 1962, 1963, 1968, 1971, 1972, 1973,
1975, 1977, and 1994 by The Lockman Foundation, La Habra, Calif. Used
by permission.

ISBN: 0-8024-4106-8

5 7 9 10 8 6 4

Printed in the United States of America

To Jan Meeks—from Danny

Second only to a personal relationship with Jesus Christ, the greatest treasure a man can have is a woman who truly loves him. I thank the Lord for the awesome treasure you are in my life.

Contents

1

The Rebirth of the *Daystar*

Red alert! Red alert! All hands to battle stations!"

Raina St. Clair roused out of a sound sleep with a sudden jerk. The shrill alarm that blared over the communications system into her small cabin brought her rolling off the bunk, and for a moment she stood looking around in confusion.

Then the harsh call to battle stations blasted through the *Daystar* again. As she rapidly pulled on her uniform, Raina wondered what emergency had arisen.

There was no time to comb the auburn hair that curled over her head. She jammed her feet into her boots and rushed out of the cabin. As she dashed down the passageway, she saw her companions falling out of their cabins and heading for their battle stations.

"What is it, Raina?" Ringo Smith was a small boy of fourteen, weighing no more than a hundred and twenty-five pounds. His brown hair was awry, and his eyes were wide with alarm.

"I don't know, Ringo."

They turned down another passage, and Raina ran headlong into Hector Jordan, who was knocked flat on the deck.

Heck's face flushed almost to match his red hair. "Why don't you watch where you're going!" The overweight boy scrambled to his feet, looking at them reproachfully. "You could hurt a fellow like that! I've got to be careful of my body!"

Raina shot him a disgusted look, scrambled to her feet too, and said, "Come on, Ringo!"

They left Heck, grumbling and moving on toward his own battle station.

Almost falling over one another, Raina and Ringo entered the bridge area.

Due to the refit of *Daystar*, the new bridge was much more modern and spacious than the previous one. Rectangular in design instead of oval, it allowed the refit team to install three main view screens. The largest, the center screen, featured the main view. The screen to the right of the main viewer was designed for weapons and tactical information. The screen on the left provided navigational information. The captain's station, located at the rear center of the bridge, gave him a good vantage point to view his bridge crew and the three forward screens.

One large center console was positioned halfway between the captain's station and the forward view screens. This console was used by the helmsman, the navigator, and the weapons officers. Behind the console stood Capt. Mark Edge, disgust written on his face. He was a tall man, over six feet, and his blue-gray eyes glinted like laser beams.

"We were just destroyed by Zonairan gunships!" he thundered. "You two were not at your stations at the allotted time. You are responsible for the death of every person aboard the *Daystar!*"

Ringo turned pale and dropped his head. A rather shy boy, he apparently could not think of a thing to say. Although he was an expert on a computer, he was physically not very agile and was well aware of that.

Raina St. Clair, who served in communications with First Officer Zeno Thrax on the *Daystar*, had a more militant spirit. She straightened up, and her light green eyes met the captain's fully. She said evenly, "It was only a drill, Captain."

"Only a drill!" Captain Edge looked like an ancient Viking as he threw up his hands in despair. "That's what I get for hiring a nursery to run a space cruiser! I knew it would never work!"

Raina thought of how she and the other ensigns aboard the *Daystar* had come to serve under Captain Edge. They had all been expelled from the Intergalactic Academy, and Edge had recruited them as part of his crew for a mission to the planet Makon. All of them had been so young that Edge and the rest of the crew were doubtful. But Raina believed they had proved their worth on the voyage, for the Makon mission had been highly successful.

"I'm sorry, Captain," she said quietly. "We'll do better the next time."

"You'll have to," Edge grumbled. He ran his hand through his light blond hair. "I've made a decision. We're going to give a more military look to this ship. I know we're not part of the Galactic Star Squadron, but from now on we're going to run this ship as if you were ensigns aboard one of their space cruisers."

"I think that would be very good, Captain." Raina nodded instantly, for she was basically an agreeable, mild-mannered girl. Glancing over at Ringo, she saw that he was humiliated by their failure, and as soon as Captain Edge dismissed them, she said, "Don't worry about it, Ringo."

"He was really sore, wasn't he?"

"You know Captain Edge. He wants everything done perfectly."

"But he's not perfect himself!" Ringo Smith glanced resentfully toward the captain, who was now engaged in bawling out Ivan Petroski, the chief engineer. "I don't see why he has to be so hard on us."

"Well, after all, we *are* young—even younger than he is—and we have to prove ourselves."

"I thought we proved ourselves on that voyage to Makon!" Ringo said shortly.

Ringo looked undersized in his uniform, which consisted of a slate gray tunic with silver trim on the collar and sleeves. The rank insignia of Ensign was affixed to the lower right sleeve near the wrist. Charcoal gray pants and boots finished off the *Daystar* Ensigns' military-looking uniform.

A gold medal hung around his neck, covered by his tunic, but Raina knew it was there. It was the only identification he had, for he had been found abandoned and placed in a state orphanage. Raina sensed that his hard upbringing had made him distrustful, and she had tried to show an extra amount of compassion toward Ringo. But he remained withdrawn, and she had almost given up.

Back on the bridge, Captain Edge dismissed Petroski and turned to Commander Zeno Thrax, his first officer. Edge was still not happy with the emergency drill. "I don't know what we're going to do with these babies, Zeno."

"Actually, I think they performed very well, Captain."

Zeno Thrax was a perfect albino with white hair and colorless eyes. Although rather chilling to look upon, he was actually a warm and compassionate individual. There was an air of loneliness about him, however, for he was cut off from his people. Even Edge did not know how it had happened, but the first officer had somehow disgraced himself on his home planet, Mentor

Seven. He was, however, an excellent officer, perfectly capable of operating the *Daystar.* He did have one habit that irritated Captain Edge considerably—Thrax seemed almost able to read people's thoughts.

"You always defend them, Zeno. Why's that?"

Zeno shrugged his shoulders, and his pale eyes drifted over to where Ringo and Raina stood at their stations. "I think they have it in them to be excellent officers."

"I'm glad you think so," Edge said grumpily, "but I'm not so sure."

Then Zeno said, "Sir, I'd like to show you some of the innovations that were made while you were away."

"All right. Let's have it."

The captain and Zeno left the bridge and headed aft through the main corridor.

Thrax continued, "I know you're already impressed with the changes we made on the bridge. There's almost twice the area, and the navigation, helmsman, and weapons consoles have been combined into that one large center console."

"I must admit, I *am* very impressed. Being able to view navigations and tactical on either side of the main viewer is a major improvement, too. The new bridge design reminds me of the bridge setup on the Intergalactic Rangers' Magnum Deep Space Cruisers. Commandant Lee is sparing no expense on this refit."

Zeno ran his finger across the corridor bulkhead paint. "This is almost dry." He looked back at Edge. "Commandant Lee wants this new ship to look like the old *Daystar*, but the parts that were destroyed cannot be replaced. You'll find that the basic superstructure is the same, though, along with the engines and most of the engineering. The whole ship is larger than before."

The two officers entered the communications and

sensor computer room. The subsystem computers down linked from the mainframe were state of the art. Zeno pointed to different components in the room. "As you can see, not only have most of the electronics and computers been completely replaced, but they have also been modified by Ringo and Heck."

"How are they doing with the main computer?" Edge asked as they walked into the main computer room.

Ringo and Heck had several panels off the main computer and were working on many circuit boards.

Captain Edge grimaced when he saw Heck. "Remind me to speak to Heck about wearing his uniform."

Zeno smiled. "The ability of these kids is something to behold." He looked earnestly at the captain. "I don't know how you did it, but you managed to find virtual experts in their fields. Some of the technology they're using goes way over my head—and I keep up on things!" Thrax scratched his right bicep. "It makes me wonder why they were kicked out of the Academy."

Edge looked at the two boys working feverishly on the main computer. "I don't know, either—not really. I do know that they're different from the rest of those Academy spoiled brats. Every one of them has had a hard life—no silver spoons in any of their mouths!"

Zeno reached over and touched Edge's arm. "Let's go down to engineering. Ivan's installing brand-new phase inducers. I've never seen him so happy. He says no one will be able to catch us with the new Mark V Star Drives."

When the tour was over, the captain said, "Let's go to my cabin and have something to drink."

"Yes, sir. That would be fine."

Back in the captain's cabin, Edge said, "What will you have, Zeno?"

"If you have any cider, I would enjoy that."

"You still like that stuff? I can't bear it."

Thrax had developed a taste for an earth drink called apple cider and had included it among their supplies.

Edge went over to a small wet bar and found a bottle of cider, then poured himself something else.

The two men sat back and relaxed awhile. Thrax was tired. It had been a hard job refitting the *Daystar*, for the ship had been almost destroyed in the battle with Sir Richard Irons's powerful cruiser.

"You've done a good job, Zeno," Captain Edge murmured. He switched on some music, a symphony performed on glass drums that had a particularly delicate reverberation. He hummed the melody and then turned to his first officer.

"I've been thinking, Zeno. We've got to get away from here and get back to Makon."

"We don't know, sir, what Commandant Lee's orders will be."

The answer clearly displeased Edge. He picked up a small object from the table beside him and tossed it into the air. It was a tiny skull that looked humanoid, but Thrax knew it was of a miniature ape that they had encountered on the planet Zonair. Thrax did not like the idea of the skull, for he had been fond of the tiny apes, but he said nothing.

"If we get away before she gives us the orders," Edge said abruptly, "then she can't issue a recall. Or if she does, we can have—" he grinned "—radio failure."

"I don't think that's very wise, Captain," Zeno said. "You want to be rich, don't you?"

Edge put down the small skull and frowned. "I wish you wouldn't do that—you don't know how it irritates me to have someone rummaging around through my thoughts."

"I'm sorry, Captain. I really can't help it."

"Yes, you could. You do it on purpose."

Thrax did not argue with the captain, but he well knew that up until recently Capt. Mark Edge had been little more than a pirate. He had built the *Daystar* out of junk parts and stolen the drive design from Sir Richard Irons to make it capable of space voyages. Then he had alienated the inhabitants of Makon by stealing some of their diamondlike mineral tridium.

Captain Edge said, "All we have to do is get back, get some tridium, and bring it back to Earth. You wouldn't believe the money I've been offered for it."

"Yes, I would believe you, Captain." The industrial galaxy was in need of such a diamondlike mineral.

"Well, I do want to be rich."

Thrax thought about this for a moment, and he said, "I don't really desire that, Captain Edge."

Edge snapped, "Well, I do!"

Rising to his feet, the captain drained the rest of his drink, then said, "Come along, Zeno. We're going to prepare for a training mission." He grinned. "And we might as well make it to Makon as anywhere else. We do need to have a breaking in of the new *Daystar.*"

Knowing well what was on his captain's mind, Zeno Thrax bobbed his head slightly but said nothing. He was thinking, *I wish he weren't so anxious to be rich. It's going to get him into trouble—and maybe all the rest of us.*

Jerusha Ericson stretched and then leaned over and touched her toes. At fifteen, she was an attractive girl with ash blonde hair and very dark blue eyes set in a squarish face. At five ten she was taller than most girls and had a strong, athletic body. Straightening up, she looked over toward the delicate teenager who was sitting on the opposite bunk, reading from a small book monitor.

"You're always reading, Mei-Lani." Jerusha grinned. "And you never forget anything."

"Oh, yes, I forget many things."

Mei-Lani Lao was only an inch over five feet and weighed five pounds less than a hundred. She was pure oriental with jet black hair and almond-shaped brown eyes. There was a quiet, reserved air about her. She smiled over at the tall girl who was watching her and said, "I wouldn't like for the captain to know how many things I do forget."

Jerusha dropped onto the bunk across from Mei-Lani, pulled her feet up, and sat cross-legged. She was wearing a simple blue tunic today that matched her eyes, and now she picked up a brush and began to brush her long hair. "If you've ever forgotten anything, I don't know what it was."

She studied the young woman, trying to pick up on the emotions inside the small body. Jerusha Ericson was unusually insightful. She was no mind reader, but she was keenly sensitive to the emotions of people. As she watched Mei-Lani's eyes going over the tiny screen, Jerusha thought, *I've never met anybody with as much peace as Mei-Lani. I wish I had that much.*

Mei-Lani looked up. "You're worried about the captain, aren't you?"

The observation troubled Jerusha, but she sensed no animosity or anything of the sort in Mei-Lani. "Well, I *am* somewhat afraid of the way he's going."

Mei-Lani put down the book monitor and gave her full attention to her friend. Her side of the cabin was filled with objects of all sorts. She loved to collect all kinds of things—from minerals from Pluto to an ancient Chinese scroll that dated all the way back to the third century B.C. Everything was neatly arranged and catalogued.

Something in the scroll had always intrigued Jerusha, as if someone were calling from ages past. It was only a fleeting thought—like a voice in the wind.

Mei-Lani let her eyes run over the scroll, then back to Jerusha. "Can I say something, Jerusha?"

"Why, of course you can."

"I think you're too . . ." Mei-Lani seemed to have trouble putting her thoughts into words. Then she said, "I think you're too interested in the captain."

"Why, that's ridiculous!"

She knew the denial came too quickly.

"I think you have what people used to call a *crush* on Captain Edge."

"A crush? I never heard of such a thing." Jerusha wielded the brush with too much force, then tossed it aside and began braiding her hair. Her fingers moved very fast. She was evasive as she said, "Naturally, I admire the captain. I think he's very able."

"Don't fool yourself, Jerusha."

"I'm not fooling myself."

"It isn't unusual for girls to become infatuated with good-looking older guys. There have been many novels written about it, and I've seen it myself."

"You're usually very smart about people, Mei-Lani, but you're wrong this time. I'm just worried about him, that's all. He wants to be rich, and I'm afraid it'll get us into trouble if that doesn't change."

Jerusha came off her bunk, knowing Mei-Lani could tell that she was upset by the conversation. "I'm going to work out with Lieutenant Jaleel."

"Well, be careful she doesn't break your neck. She doesn't know her own strength, and she forgets that martial arts can hurt people."

"She can't hurt me!"

Mei-Lani said, "That's the trouble with you, Jerusha. You don't think anyone can hurt you—but you could be wrong about that."

The fleeting voice again beckoned Jerusha as she started to leave Mei-Lani's cabin—just a whisper that seemed to say, *Apart from Me you can do nothing.*

Jerusha turned back in frustration and looked at Mei-Lani. "What is that scroll about, anyway?"

Mei-Lani stood and walked over to the scroll. "The words are from the Old Testament—Second Kings, chapter six—where an army is sent to kill the old prophet Elijah. But God sent a spiritual army to protect His servant. Elijah knew that without God he could do nothing. But with God all things are possible."

Ivan Petroski was arguing with Heck Jordan. That was not unusual, for the two often argued. Petroski was no more than four and a half feet tall but was well proportioned, with brown eyes and thick brown hair. He came from the planet Bellinka, where all the people were small.

Petroski glared at Heck, who today was wearing a combination of colors that was almost blinding. He had dredged up a bright yellow tunic and beneath it wore a pair of purple, tightfitting trousers. He had some sort of reptilian belt around his pudgy stomach, and, as usual, he was eating.

"If you can stop eating long enough, Ensign Jordan, I'd like to have a little help here."

"Why, sure, Chief," Heck said.

Petroski knew the fifteen-year-old was an electronics genius. But Heck spent more time thinking about clothes and girls than about his business, which irritated everybody. He was also a wheeler-dealer, very sneaky at times, and ultimately selfish. Now he tossed away the core of the passion fruit that he had been eating. It missed the wastebasket.

Petroski said, "Pick that up!"

"What are you so touchy about?" Heck complained. "Anybody can miss a wastebasket."

Petroski scowled. "We're going on a shakedown cruise, and I want the computer system on this ship to be perfect. Do you hear me?" he asked shrilly. "Perfect!"

"Perfect like me?"

"No. Far better than that. And whoever told you you were perfect, Heck?"

"Why, I just take a look in the mirror, and there I stand." Heck grinned broadly. "Don't worry about the computer system. It's already in first-class shape, and it'll be better by the time—" He was interrupted as Ringo Smith came in.

"We just got a message from Commandant Lee. She's coming right away."

"Whatever she says won't make the captain happy unless she sends us to Makon," Heck said. "That's not a bad idea, to go to Makon. We can all get rich if we can just get some of that tridium back to Earth."

Ringo Smith shook his head. "I don't think Commandant Lee rebuilt the *Daystar* to make Captain Edge rich!"

2

Problems in the Galaxy

The *Daystar* Ensigns lined up in military formation along with the rest of the crew in order to greet Commandant Winona Lee.

Looking up at the spaceship that was coming in for a smooth landing, Raina said out of the side of her mouth, "That's some ship, isn't it, Ringo? I've never seen one like it this close."

"Neither have I, but I guess the Commandant of the Intergalactic Council deserves it."

Commandant Winona Lee's ship hovered over the landing site. The craft was a Magnum Class Deep Space Cruiser and the flagship of the entire fleet. The heavy cruiser dwarfed the *Daystar* like the whale about to swallow Jonah.

Raina said, "Beside that, the *Daystar* looks like a grasshopper." She glanced over at her friends. Each of them had his jaw hanging open in awe.

The commandant's cruiser was more than twenty stories high, 700 meters long, and 300 meters from port to starboard. She was divided into three sections: the bow, the fuselage, and the engine section, located aft of the fuselage.

A large bubble atop the bow was the bridge area. Her forward section hung low like a great upside-down skyscraper full of sensor arrays, turbo cannon, and the primary communications array. The fuselage connecting the bow with the stern was only fifty meters in diameter but extended 300 meters in length. The aft engine section was designed as a cube that was half the size of the bow. This area housed the main reactor, aft sensor unit, and deflector shield generator. It also incorporated static discharge rods for atmospheric travel. The engines on this ship were the largest known to exist.

As the cruiser neared the surface, large bolts of electricity shot up from the ground, attacking the static discharge rods.

"I'm glad I'm nowhere near that!" Heck said quietly.

Raina didn't doubt that Heck had been shocked many times as he worked on his computers, but the voltage they were looking at now would incinerate him in a split second.

The electrical fireworks display came to a halt, and the spaceship's landing arms swung down. A voice came over the intercom speakers: *"Pegasus to Daystar."*

Captain Edge responded quizzically, *"Daystar* here. Go ahead, Captain Pursey." Edge looked around at his young crew, then at his small ship, little more than a fancied-up freighter, and asked himself, *With a ship that size and with all that power—why does he need our help?*

Pursey's deep voice was smooth yet resonated with authority. "Commandant Lee will be at your ship shortly. Prepare to greet Her Excellency."

After the ship landed, there were a few moments' pause. Then a part of the side of the craft seemed to disappear, and a woman came walking down the ramp that had suddenly projected outward.

"Attention!" Mark Edge called out and looked down the line to be sure that the military formation was suitable. He stepped forward and saluted the woman, who stopped and returned his salute.

Commandant Winona Lee was a small woman with silver hair and mild gray eyes. As Commandant of the Intergalactic Council she was one of the most powerful individuals in the galaxy, although nothing about her appearance seemed to suggest this.

"Welcome to the new *Daystar*, Commandant."

"Thank you, Captain Edge."

"How do you like the new uniforms?"

Commandant Lee's eyes went over the crew. "Very smart, indeed." She moved down the line of ensigns, greeting each by name. It was a way she had of making those under her feel important. Even Ringo Smith stood a little straighter when she took his hand and said, "Well, Ensign Smith, it's good to see you again. I've thought about you often since our last meeting."

"You have?" Ringo blushed. "I've thought about you, too, Commandant Lee."

After the inspection of the crew, Captain Edge said, "Ensign Ericson, we will have the commandant at our noon mess."

"Certainly, Captain. I'll see to it at once." Jerusha saluted and, motioning, disappeared in the company of Mei-Lani and Raina St. Clair.

For the next two hours the commandant went over the refurbished ship carefully. She asked penetrating questions, which Edge, Chief Petroski, and Zeno Thrax fielded skillfully. When she got to Lieutenant Tara Jaleel, the weapons officer, she looked up at the tall woman and smiled. "Lieutenant Jaleel, I'm happy to see you again. Are you satisfied with the armament of the new ship?"

Edge smiled too, for Tara Jaleel was never satisfied with anything. She was a Masai woman with roots going back to an African tribe noted for their fierce ways. She was almost six feet tall, but her face was attractive despite her rather fierce look.

"I am working to improve everything, especially our turbo cannons. I want to be able to knock anything that comes at us out of the sky."

"I'll hope that your next mission won't involve anything like that," Commandant Lee said. "But I'm happy you're aboard the ship. I feel safe with you in charge of security and weapons."

As they left, Captain Edge said enviously, "I wish I knew how to handle people like you do, Commandant."

"By the time you're as old as I am, you will have made all your mistakes—and if you're still living after that, you will know people better."

Edge nodded respectfully.

At that moment Jerusha reappeared, saying, "The meal is ready, Captain, when you are."

"And I'm starved," Commandant Lee said cheerfully.

The mess hall was not large, but it had been completely remodeled. Everywhere were shining stainless steel tables, and chairs padded with attractive maroon leather taken from an ox that was raised only on the planet Dernof. It wore like iron but was exceptionally soft.

As Winona Lee settled herself into her chair and looked over the array of food, her eyes rose to Jerusha's. "Ensign Ericson, are you responsible for this meal?"

Jerusha returned her smile. "Ensigns Lao and St. Clair joined with me. It's a joint effort, you might say."

When all the officers and ensigns had taken their places, Commandant Lee said, "You don't have a chaplain."

"Why, no, we don't," Edge admitted.

22

"Then I suppose you'll have to ask the blessing yourself, Captain Edge."

The request caught Edge off guard. He was not a praying man, although he did try to be an honorable one—most of the time. His eyes leaped up to meet Jerusha's. She was covering a smile with her hand. He knew she was laughing at him. In fact, he suspected that the commandant too was amused at his embarrassment.

He said, "I delegate that task to one of the ensigns. They need all the practice they can get. Ensign St. Clair, ask the blessing—and make it a *short* one."

Raina bowed her head and said simply, "Lord, we thank You for this food, for our guest, and for every blessing which You have sent. In the name of Jesus give us safety and draw us ever nearer to You. Amen."

"Amen," Winona Lee said.

And now the commandant turned her attention to the meal. When her plate was filled, she said, "I don't believe I recognize some of these dishes, Ensign Ericson."

"Oh, Mei-Lani picked out the menu," Jerusha said. "Mei-Lani, why don't you tell the commandant what she's eating?"

Mei-Lani smiled shyly, but there was excitement in her brown eyes. Everyone knew she loved to cook. She said, "That dish on your right is bird's nest soup."

Winona Lee blinked. "Bird's nest soup?" she asked with apprehension.

"Oh, it's very good," Mei-Lani said. "It's been a dish of my people for centuries. The dish right beside it is octopus."

"You mean the creature with so many legs?"

"Yes. Very young and very tender. They're delicious," Mei-Lani said. "And the bread is made from a

23

grain that grows only on a small area in what used to be Kansas. I think you'll like it, Commandant."

The commandant said, "I'm sure I will."

As they began to eat, Heck Jordan piled his plate so high that it appeared to be a small mountain. Irrepressibly, he said, "Commandant Lee, you ought to try some of this." He lifted a bottle of some red substance.

"What is that, Ensign Jordan?"

"It's *picante* sauce. That means 'hot.' It puts real flavor into it." He baptized his own food with a liberal layer of the sauce so that the food itself was almost invisible.

But when he attempted to pass the sauce to the commandant, she shook her head.

"I think it might be a little warm for me."

"Be too warm for anybody except for Heck." The captain grinned. He winked at Jerusha, adding, "It's so hot it's destroyed all his taste buds. He doesn't taste anything now."

"I certainly do!" Heck said indignantly.

The meal went on, and they were eating a delicious fruit dessert that Raina had made when the captain rose to say, "I'd like to propose a toast to—"

He never finished his toast, for something struck him in the back, hard. Off balance, he fell forward, sprawling awkwardly across the table. Dishes clattered, hardware went everywhere, and despite himself, Edge's face slapped down into the bowl of the dessert, which had a large helping of whipped cream on it.

Edge yelped and rolled over—and found his shoulders bearing a heavy weight. He looked up into the eyes of the very large female German shepherd that belonged to Jerusha.

"Get away from me, you beast!" He pushed, but the dog was too heavy. "Jerusha, get this animal off me!"

24

"Contessa, out!"

Contessa stopped licking the cream off Edge's face and raised her head. She was a massive animal, a kind of super German shepherd, bred for intelligence. As a rule she did not like people except for Jerusha, but somehow she had become enamored of Captain Edge.

Edge detested her. He did not like dogs at all.

"Out, Contessa!" Jerusha repeated sharply.

Edge watched as the large dog dropped to all fours and trotted out of the dining room. Food was all over the captain's tunic and creamed fruit on his face. He felt like an absolute fool.

He glared at Jerusha. "You'll hear about this, Ensign Ericson!" Then, with as much dignity as he could muster, he said, "Excuse me, Commandant. I'll go change clothes." He hesitated, then added, "Now you see what the captain of a ship has to put up with when the ensigns are all *infants!*"

When the captain was gone, Jerusha said, "I'm so sorry, Commandant. It was all my fault."

"Is that your dog?"

"Yes, I've had her since she was born. She's very smart, and she saved some lives when we were on our mission to Makon." Jerusha tried not to smile then. "She doesn't like many people, but she loves Captain Edge. She can't stay away from him."

"Captain Edge obviously doesn't return the feeling."

"Oh, he'll get used to her," Heck said airily. "I'll give him some lessons on how to win a dog's favor."

Commandant Lee turned her cool gray eyes on Heck Jordan. "I assume you have had special training in this, Ensign Jordan."

"Well, no. But after all, there can't be all that much to it."

Ringo whispered into Jerusha's ear. "Does he have to talk like that to the commandant?"

"It's just his way," Jerusha said. She laid a hand on Ringo's arm. "Don't let it bother you."

The captain came back in ten minutes wearing a fresh uniform. He gave Jerusha a sharp glance but then turned to the commandant.

"Were you happy with the ship, Your Excellency?"

"Yes. The renovations all seem to be very good."

She looked around the table. Those present included the ensigns, Zeno Thrax of the regular crew, and a small lady who had said nothing during the meal. This was Bronwen Llewellen, the navigator. An older woman, she had been a space pioneer. At first Edge had refused to accept her but was now happy that he had, for she had piloted the *Daystar* through difficult positions to find Makon.

Beside Bronwen sat her nephew, Dai Bando, now an ensign as well. At sixteen, he was the oldest of the young people. Almost six feet tall, with a perfect build, he possessed tremendous physical skills, strength, agility, and speed. He was not as bright as the other ensigns, but he had other talents that the captain had learned to appreciate.

To Dai's left sat Tara Jaleel, his weapons officer. She now spoke up. "What is our mission going to be, Commandant, if I might ask?"

Commandant Lee said, "I think it's time I shared that with you. Thank you for reminding me, Lieutenant Jaleel. I've had such an enjoyable meal with you, I put off telling you as long as possible."

"Sounds like a difficult mission, Commandant," Edge said, his eyes narrowing. "I was hoping we could go back to Makon."

"I'm afraid that will not be possible, at least not for now."

"Oh," Edge said, trying to cover his disappointment.

Commandant Lee studied him, then said, "There is a very difficult situation which has arisen on the planet Merlina."

Edge frowned. "Merlina? I don't know that one."

"I do," Mei-Lani said. "It's on the far outskirts of the galaxy. I have studied it quite extensively."

"Then you know, Ensign Lao, something about its history," Commandant Lee said.

"I know that the colonists' history is involved with some sort of sorcery. If I remember correctly," Mei-Lani said, thinking hard, "they named their planet after a magician named Merlin, a mythological figure back in English history."

"That is correct. They are not very advanced mechanically and technically, but apparently they are skilled in expertise of a different sort."

"I don't believe in magic!" Tara Jaleel snapped. "It's all superstition."

"I'd like to think so, Lieutenant Jaleel," Winona Lee said calmly, "but the evidence is all to the contrary. It appears that these people have developed some sort of terrible spiritual powers. As a matter of fact, we don't know too much about it, but we do know they have taken over several small planets in their sector—all without complex scientific weapons."

Raina St. Clair said, "May I ask a question, Commandant?"

"Why, certainly, Ensign."

"These people are dabblers in the dark arts of witchcraft?"

"I think that is exactly the case," Winona Lee said.

Again Tara Jaleel insisted, "And I don't believe in witchcraft. It's not scientific."

"No, it certainly isn't. But whatever it is that these people do is very powerful."

Bronwen Llewellen spoke up. "I assume you will want us to travel to Merlina, Commandant Lee."

"Yes. Will you have trouble with the navigation?"

"No, I think not, but we had difficulty on our last voyage for lack of a surgeon."

Winona Lee frowned. "That's right. You did not have a surgeon."

"So we can't go there. Right away, at least," Edge broke in quickly. "What about if we made one quick trip to Makon? Just a shakedown cruise, Commandant. In the meanwhile you can find a surgeon for us. Then, when we come back, we'll be ready for the mission to Merlina."

A small smile touched the commandant's lips. "That will not be necessary, Captain. It occurs to me that I already have just the person for you."

"You do?" Edge asked. He knew he was not hiding his disappointment this time.

"Yes." Commandant Lee took a sip of water, then looked around. "And there will be no time for a shake-down cruise for the *Daystar*. You will leave for Merlina immediately." She turned to Edge. "Tomorrow, Captain, Dr. Cole will report, and your crew will be complete. I will expect you to leave as soon as the doctor is aboard and ready."

3

"Gentleness Is Important, Too"

Ringo broke into a cold sweat but raised his hands in a position of defense. Over and over again, Lieutenant Tara Jaleel had instructed him on how to protect himself against attack from an enemy. Now as the tall woman circled him, her eyes glittering, a streak of fear ran through Ringo.

Lieutenant Jaleel believed that pain made a person better, and therefore she inflicted as much damage as she legitimately could on her pupils as she taught them martial arts. Some of the bruises that Ringo had suffered from his last lesson had not yet faded, and now he gritted his teeth and wished that he were anywhere in the world but in the gymnasium facing Tara Jaleel.

Suddenly she uttered a shrill cry and shot forward. Ringo threw up his left arm to block the blow. But faster than he could move, Lieutenant Jaleel threw herself upright and lashed out with both feet. Her heels caught Ringo in the stomach. His breath came out with a *whoosh,* and he pitched backwards. The back of his head struck the padded bulkhead with a thud, and he collapsed to the floor, trying desperately to take in a breath. He was still gasping when Jaleel came over and glared down at him.

"I told you, Ensign Smith, never expect the expected! You thought I would come at you with my right-hand blow, so all I had to do was change to a solar plexus strike with the feet."

Ringo's breath sounded hoarse and raspy in the silence of the gymnasium. It was a relatively small room but big enough for Jaleel to bring her pupils and teach them how to protect themselves—and how to hurt other people.

Jaleel seized the front of Ringo's loose white jacket and pulled him to his feet as if he weighed nothing. She held him there, almost on tiptoe, saying, "All right. Let's try it again."

"I think that's enough for now, don't you, Lieutenant?"

Jaleel whirled.

Raina St. Clair had entered. She was wearing the loose-fitting white uniform of the martial arts students. Her hair was tied up carefully. She wore no makeup, but still there was high color in her cheeks and lips. She had light green eyes, beautiful auburn hair—with a widow's peak—and a dimple in her chin. Ringo thought she looked rather frail when contrasted with the athletic form of Tara Jaleel.

He knew Jaleel did not like Raina—that she considered the girl to be soft. *Too religious. Not be worth anything in a fight*, Jaleel had told the captain. But now, if she hoped to intimidate Raina with her iron gaze, Raina simply met her stare.

"You're a fine one to talk, Miss St. Clair!" Jaleel snapped. "You haven't progressed an inch since I started trying to teach you the art of Jain Jayati. You must learn how to defend yourself and how to attack."

Raina continued to gaze at the fire that raged in Tara's eyes. "I know you think that Jain Jayati is an excellent discipline for us to learn, but I don't think you realize that Jain Jayati was birthed in darkness—and that darkness has a strong hold on you."

Jaleel snapped back, "Child, don't push your religious beliefs on me. I am the instructor here—and you will do as I say, *Ensign* St. Clair."

Then it was Ringo's turn to watch as Raina took her punishment. Small and light-boned, she had no chance at all against the lightning-hard blows of the weapons officer. Time and time again Jaleel knocked Raina backward. She did not succeed, however, in causing her to cry out, for no matter how hard Jaleel struck, Raina never made a sound.

Finally Jaleel stopped, afraid perhaps of getting a reprimand from the captain for being too rough, as she already had on several occasions. "You two will never amount to anything!"

Raina was trying to get her breath. Her face was pale. But she said mildly, "You ought to have more in your life than fighting, Lieutenant Jaleel."

"Nothing is more important than fighting!"

Raina shook her head. "But what will happen when you are too old to fight?"

"That will never happen! I will die in battle!" Jaleel gave the two a withering glance and stalked out without a backward look.

Ringo said, "You shouldn't argue with her, Raina. It just makes it worse."

"I feel sorry for her."

"Sorry for *her?* What about me? And what about yourself? And what about poor Heck? Before you came, she beat him so badly he could barely walk when he left here."

"She's not a happy woman. I mean, all she knows is fighting and violence and weapons. What do you think that does to a person? No kindness, no gentleness, no goodness. She's afraid to let those things out —afraid someone would think she isn't tough."

"Well, *I'll* never think that." Ringo rubbed his stomach tenderly. "I'll be sore for a week after that kick she gave me. In order to be fair, she ought to give us a baseball bat or something."

Raina consoled Ringo as best she could, and, later that day, as she went about her duties at the communications station, she thought about what had happened. By the time she went off duty, she'd made a decision. She went to Captain Edge's cabin, touched the button, and heard his voice say, "Enter."

Stepping inside, she found Edge standing before a set of astro maps. He turned to face her and asked suspiciously, "You don't have Ensign Ericson's dog with you, do you?"

"Contessa? No."

"Good. I hate that animal!"

"But she loves you so much, Captain."

"I can't help that. I'm going to run off and leave her behind, if possible." He wagged his head in disgust, then said, "What is it, Ensign St. Clair?"

"I would like to talk to you about a problem, Captain."

"You too? Everybody on the ship's been here with a problem. What's yours?"

"It's about Lieutenant Jaleel, sir. I think she treats Ensign Jordan and Ensign Smith much too roughly."

Quickly Edge's eyes ran over the girl. She saw that he spotted the bruise on the side of her neck. He came over and touched it lightly. "Where did you get that?"

"I—I'd rather not say."

"It looks like Jaleel's fingerprint to me. Her mark, anyway. She give you that?"

"Well, yes sir. But—"

"So you're trying to get out of your lessons."

"No, I'm not, Captain. I'm not complaining for myself. But—well, you see, Ringo and Heck both have some other deep-seated problems. Especially Ringo."

"What's wrong with *him?*"

Raina thought for a moment how much she could tell the captain. "He's had a terrible life. He doesn't know who he is."

"What do you mean, he doesn't know who he is?"

"I mean, he was found on the doorstep of a state orphanage."

"Was there a note or anything like that?"

"No sir. Only a medallion around his neck. A gold medallion with the image of a man's face on one side and some words on the other that he can't read." Raina's eyes turned soft as she said, "I feel so sorry for him. Can you imagine how it would be not knowing your parents?"

"Well, I can't think that's any worse than your own background. You lost your parents in a house fire, didn't you—both at the same time?"

"Well, yes sir."

"And your father died getting you out, didn't he?"

Tears glistened in Raina's eyes, and she could not answer. Finally she swallowed and said, "Yes sir, but—"

"Then I suggest you stop feeling sorry for Smith. He's got to become a man, and that's it. As for Heck, he needs to be toughened up, too. He's overweight, and he's the smoothest operator I've ever seen. Why, he thinks he ought to be running this ship, not me."

"Well, he has problems, too, Captain. That's the reason he overeats. He really feels unaccepted."

"I'm not running a psychological clinic, Ensign! This is a space cruiser," Edge snapped. "Now, Lieutenant

Jaleel is following my orders. I told her to toughen up the crew, and that's what she's doing. That's important."

Raina hesitated for one moment more. She was aware that some of what the captain said was true. She was aware also that he was a man who needed to prove his own toughness, and she doubted that anything she could possibly say would change him. At last she said quietly, "Gentleness is important, too, Captain." Then she saluted, turned, and left the room.

Edge watched Raina St. Clair go, unable to think of a proper reply to call after her. After the door had closed, he threw down the calipers he held in his hand and said viciously, "Now I get instructions in psychotherapy! All the crew's got self-esteem problems!" Shamefacedly, he picked up the calipers, but then looked at the door. "Well, they're not the only ones, Ensign St. Clair!"

He turned back to the maps and with a troubled look began to chart a course as best he could for Merlina.

Studs Cagney, the crew chief, was working on the engine with Ivan Petroski and Jerusha Ericson. The three of them had recalibrated the Star Drive power flow actuators. They had been at it for hours, making final adjustments.

"I think it's going to be all right now—the actuators are back within specs," Jerusha said, straightening up. She had on her coveralls, which were now dirty and stained with molybdenum disulfide grease, and when she wiped her forehead she left a streak across it.

"If you don't need me anymore," Studs said, "I've got other things to do."

Studs Cagney was a huge man, short but muscular. On the trip to Makon it was learned he'd sold out to the enemy, and Lieutenant Jaleel wanted to throw him out into space. But Dai Bando promised to watch him, and the two had learned to work together.

Studs found Dai moving some equipment. He watched with his eyes narrowed as the boy walked over to a generator that, Studs knew, weighed more than two hundred pounds. He gasped as Dai picked it up and carried it across the room as if it weighed nothing. "He's got the strength of a gorilla," he muttered.

"Hello, Studs. What's happening?"

"Finally got the engines fixed. I hear we'll be lifting off as soon as that doctor gets on board."

"Have you ever been to Merlina, Studs?"

"Never been in that part of the galaxy, but I'll tell you right now, I don't like the place."

"What's wrong with it?" Dai asked. He leaned against the bulkhead, his black hair down over his forehead. The boy had intense black eyes, broad shoulders, a narrow waist, and looked like the athlete that he was. "Is it as dangerous as some of the other planets you've been to?"

"I think it's worse." Studs Cagney had been in many dangerous places. He was not afraid of monstrous beasts or of enemies with dangerous and powerful weapons, but now he rubbed his finger over his thick, broken nose and said, "I just don't like it."

"Never knew you to be nervous about anything. What is it, Studs?"

Cagney looked at him. "Well, I ain't been there, but there's been lots of rumors about that place. It's full of spooks."

"Spooks?" Dai grinned, and two dimples appeared, one in each cheek. "What do you mean, *spooks?*"

"I mean there's a bunch there called 'the wizards.' They know how to call up ghosts and put spells on people. Oh, I've heard about 'em, and I don't relish none of it, you bet."

Dai studied him. "Well, it'll be an interesting trip."

About the time that Dai was talking with Studs, Jerusha ran into the captain.

He looked at her and grinned. "Your face is dirty."

Involuntarily Jerusha reached up and touched her cheek and left another streak.

"Now it's dirtier still. Here, let me clean it off."

Reaching into his pocket, Edge produced a handkerchief and wiped at the grease on Jerusha's face. "Won't come off that way. My, you are a dirty girl!"

Jerusha glared and said furiously, "It's impossible to keep clean when you're working on an engine."

"I know, Jerusha. I was just teasing." He frowned then. "I hope this Dr. Cole turns out to be a drunk or maybe a hundred-year-old man. Somebody we couldn't possibly take."

"Why do you wish that?" But immediately Jerusha knew. "Oh, I see!"

With surprise Edge looked at her. "What do you mean, you *see?* You read minds?"

"No, I just can sense that you are very angry, and you don't want to go on this trip because you want to go to Makon and get tridium—and make a lot of money."

"You're as bad as Zeno Thrax! I thought you couldn't read minds."

"I can't, Captain. But I do know you're angry, and you've made no secret about wanting to go back to Makon. You said as much to Commandant Lee."

"Well, it wouldn't hurt her to let us make that one

trip. This other business could wait. Anyway, I hope the doctor turns out to be a dud. Somebody I can legitimately refuse."

As they walked down through the ship, Jerusha thought about what Mei-Lani had said. She stole a glance at Captain Edge, and thought, *He's the best-looking man I've ever seen, though he doesn't seem to know it. I'll say that for him. But Mei-Lani's wrong.*

Beside her, Edge continued to verbally explore ways to get rid of the new doctor. Without even having seen the physician, it was clear that he was ready to find any excuse to get rid of him. Suddenly the communicator on his belt said, "Bridge to Captain!"

"Edge here."

"Captain, Dr. Cole has come aboard, reporting for duty."

"I'll be right there."

Turning the communicator off, Edge grinned crookedly at Jerusha. "Come along. You can help me find some reason for getting rid of this sawbones."

On the bridge Zeno Thrax met them. "I asked the doctor to wait in the war room."

"Thank you, First. OK, Jerusha. Let's get rid of this fellow."

Jerusha followed closely behind the captain. When he opened the door to the war room, he stopped so abruptly that she ran into him. "Oh, I'm sorry, Captain," she said.

The captain did not answer but stood stock-still. Jerusha stepped aside so that she could see around him, knowing that he was, for some reason, struck by something about the reporting surgeon. As soon as she took one look, she too was stunned.

"I am Dr. Temple Cole."

The speaker was one of the most beautiful women

that Jerusha had ever seen. She seemed to be in her mid-twenties. Her hair was a strawberry color, a beautiful tint, cut short, and very curly. She had enormous violet eyes, shadowed by dark lashes, and a generously curved mouth. Her skin was creamy, and she wore a clingy light green dress. She was not what Jerusha had been expecting—nor, obviously, the captain, either.

"Ah . . . well . . . you're Dr. Cole?" Edge stammered.

"Why, yes. Didn't Commandant Lee tell you I would be reporting for duty?"

Edge seemed to have lost his ability to communicate. He floundered for a moment longer, then said, "Well, yes—I believe she did."

Jerusha touched his arm lightly.

Glancing at her, he said, "Oh, and this is our flight engineer, Ensign Jerusha Ericson."

"I'm happy to know you, Ensign." Temple Cole immediately turned back to the captain. "I understand that the plan is to leave as soon as possible."

"Well, that's what Commandant Lee would like."

"I brought my things with me, but I will need some more medical supplies, I suspect. I'm at your service, Captain."

"Well . . ." Edge took a deep breath. He could not seem to take his eyes off the woman, Jerusha noted with displeasure. She was trying to read the young doctor and, oddly, found that, try as she might, she could pick up practically nothing about Dr. Temple Cole's person. This was interesting, for she had no difficulty with most people.

She listened as the captain stood beside the doctor, talking to her.

Then Edge said. "I think you and I had better go examine the medical stores."

"But, Captain," Jerusha interrupted, "we need you to look over the changes we made to the engines . . ."

"You and Petroski do that. Work with the first officer. It's very important that we have proper medical treatment."

If Jerusha could not pick up the emotions of the new surgeon, she had no trouble reading those of her captain. Capt. Mark Edge's emotions were doing everything but sending up sky rockets.

Why, he's infatuated with this woman! Jerusha said nothing more but watched as the two left. Then she made her way slowly out of the war room and back to the bridge, where she joined Zeno Thrax.

"Did you meet the new physician?" Zeno asked politely.

"Why do you always ask these things, Zeno? You saw me go in there," Jerusha said with irritation, "and you know perfectly well what I'm thinking!"

"You're very unhappy with Dr. Cole."

"Yes, I am."

"You think she's not a competent physician?"

"I don't know anything about that. I do know one thing. The captain is acting like a silly schoolboy! Did you see that grin on his face?"

Zeno Thrax grinned himself. "Well, she's a very attractive lady. I think it would be abnormal if the captain didn't notice that."

"Notice it? He fawned on her like a puppy!" Jerusha exclaimed.

"Ensign, I think you're more troubled about the captain than about Dr. Cole."

"That's not exactly true, Zeno." Jerusha thought for a moment. "It's strange. I can pick up no sense of what she's really like. Nothing at all."

Zeno frowned and ran a hand over his pale face.

His colorless eyes turned thoughtful. "And what you mean is," he said slowly, "you don't trust people who mask their emotions."

"I certainly don't. Do you?"

Zeno shrugged. "Most of us have things we'd like to keep secret."

"But most of us don't learn how to mask things as well as that woman does. I'm afraid there's something in her past—maybe even her present—that she doesn't want known, and I'm wondering what it is."

Zeno said gently, "Jerusha, there's something in my own past that I wouldn't want any one of my friends or my fellow crew members to know about. But you don't distrust *me*."

"No, I don't, Zeno. But I've learned to know you. This woman—there's something *wrong* about her. I don't know what it is. Call it intuition maybe, but I don't trust her."

Jerusha's first impression definitely had been twofold. One, that Capt. Mark Edge was totally infatuated with the woman's beauty and, second, that Dr. Temple Cole was something other than what she appeared to be. For the next few hours, Jerusha made it a point to stay close to the captain whenever he was with the doctor, and she saw nothing to change her mind.

"I'll find out what it is," Jerusha muttered to herself, watching the two as they sat together in the lounge. "Then I'll straighten that captain out!"

4

Dr. Temple Cole

*H*ai!"

With a piercing cry, Lieutenant Jaleel struck with all her might at the youth who stood before her. She was so powerful in the science of Jain Jayati that she had never used such force either in a match or while training a pupil. Only when in actual battle, when it was a matter of life and death, had she struck this way, for such a blow could maim or kill.

But something about this boy frustrated Jaleel. She had instructed him for some time now, and never once had she been able to land a clean blow on him—certainly not to put him down as she had the other members of the younger group. Thoroughly defeating him had become an obsession, and she had lain awake many hours thinking of how she could impose her will upon Dai Bando.

This session she had tried practically everything. But no matter how hard or fast she struck, the boy's reflexes simply guided him away, so that the blow went harmlessly by. She had attacked with her feet, and that had been as useless. Anger had risen in her slowly, until finally she had launched herself forward, crying, *"Hai!"*—the signal for a death blow.

Her right hand lashed out like a striking snake, aimed for the bridge of the young man's nose. If it struck, it would break the nose and stun Bando until another blow would be easy to deliver.

But the blow did not land. The boy simply waited

until her hand was a few inches from his face. Then, with some sort of superhuman reflex, he simply moved his head so that it whistled by. Then he raised his own right hand, and Jaleel was helpless before him.

He's going to strike, and I can't stop him was the thought that flashed through Jaleel's mind.

However, the boy simply held up his fist for a few seconds, then dropped it to his side and stepped back.

Dai Bando considered his instructor, who stared back at him with anger in her dark brown eyes. "I'm a little bit tired," he said, which she knew was untrue. "Would it be all right if we didn't practice anymore, Lieutenant?"

"All right. Get out of here!"

"Yes, ma'am." Dai went to the door, then turned back and smiled. "Thank you, Lieutenant. It's been most helpful."

"Get out, I said!"

Dai went down the causeway to the ship, speaking to crew members but mostly thinking about Lieutenant Tara Jaleel. She was a puzzle to him. He knew instinctively that she did not like him, and he could not understand why.

He went to his cabin and picked up his sitar, an ancient instrument that Mei-Lani told him had evolved from the guitar in the early nineteen sixties in America. Dai hadn't argued with her, but he knew better. The sitar was a lute created by the ancient Hindus. The instrument was made of seasoned gourds and teakwood. It was much smaller than a guitar, had fourteen strings, and Dai was very good on it.

For a while he sat strumming, his fingers picking out a melody. Then he began to sing. He sang in Welsh, a language his aunt had taught him. Bronwen had told him it had been passed down to her from her grand-mother. It was a beautiful language, and as far as he knew, they were the only two in the galaxy who spoke it.

. For a time he sat, singing softly, his eyes half closed with pleasure. Then he thought again of Lieutenant Jaleel. Rising to his feet, he put the sitar back into its Persian rug styled case, closed it, and placed it on a shelf over the head of his bunk.

Then Dai made his way to the bridge, where he glanced around at the activity there before going over to where his aunt was sitting at the navigator's console. She was working the controls, and he watched for a while. The screen reflected stars. He tried to even grasp the idea of millions and millions of stars, but his aunt seemed to know every one of them. She would tell him their names, which he almost immediately forgot.

At length she turned to him with a smile and stretched her fingers. "What have you been doing, Dai?"

"I've been having my Jain Jayati lesson with Lieutenant Jaleel."

"Oh, how did it go?"

"Not very well. She doesn't like me, Aunt."

"Did you let her win, as I told you to?"

"Not exactly. I didn't let her hurt me, but then, I didn't hurt her either. And I could have, Aunt. More than once."

"I'm glad you didn't."

Dai leaned toward her, and a lock of black hair fell down over his forehead. He had dimples that appeared when he smiled, one in each cheek, but he was not smiling now. He looked puzzled. He asked earnestly, "Why doesn't she like me, Aunt Bronwen?"

"Because she doesn't like to lose. She can't beat

you, and therefore you're her enemy." Bronwen looked up affectionately at her nephew. "Besides—the obvious problem is that you're a believer in Jesus Christ. You overcome darkness with light, not with your fists. She doesn't know that she's in darkness."

"Well, that's not good. I don't have anything against her, and I've never beaten her, really."

"She can handle anyone on this ship easily—probably anyone anywhere—except you. She's never met a man or a woman that she couldn't defeat, and it's important for a woman like that to win all the time."

"I don't see why."

Bronwen reached up and touched his cheek. "Your father had dimples just like that," she said softly. Dai's father had been her only brother, and Dai knew she had loved him dearly. "You look very much like him, you know."

"Do I, Aunt?"

"Very much. He was the best man I ever knew." She smiled again and touched the other cheek. "Except for you. You'll be as good a man as he was."

"I don't see how. I'm not bright like Ringo or Heck or any of the girls. They all know things. I don't know *anything*, Aunt. I can't run a computer very well. I don't know anything about electronics." He spread his hands. "I'm just not smart."

"You're good, though, and that's more important than being smart. Besides that, you're strong and brave and fast. We need people like you." She thought a moment, then said, "It's very important that you understand Lieutenant Jaleel. You see, she's made one thing very important in her life, and that is to be the best fighter there is. And when people make anything other than God the number one thing in life, they're not going to be happy."

"Well, she's not happy; I can tell you that. She tried to—" He started to say, "She tried to kill me with a blow today," then halted abruptly.

But his aunt said, "I know. She's tried every way she can to prove her superiority. But she can't, so she's going to hurt you."

"What should I do, Aunt Bronwen?"

"Make her your friend."

"My friend? How could I do that? She doesn't even like me."

"She doesn't trust you. She doesn't trust anyone, and that's why it's important that someone teach her how to trust. You did so well with Studs Cagney. He didn't like you, either, when you first came on board."

"I guess not." The two dimples reappeared, and the lock of hair fell down over his forehead again as Dai laughed. "Studs tried to beat my head off."

"But you're friends now, aren't you? Why is that, do you suppose?"

"I don't know. Maybe because I didn't vote to throw him out the porthole."

"No, you didn't, and you stood for him. One of these days he'll become a Christian, because he'll listen to you. He will have learned to trust you, and then you can point him to Jesus."

"You think I can do that with Lieutenant Jaleel?" Dai said doubtfully.

"I think you could, if you're willing. She's a hard woman to get close to—almost like a porcupine."

"What's a porcupine?"

"A little animal that used to live on Earth. It had lots of spiky things all over its body. You couldn't touch porcupines, or they would ram the spikes into your hand."

"Well, that sounds like Lieutenant Jaleel."

45

"It does now, but she doesn't have to be like that always. Will you try?"

"To be a friend? Sure I will, Aunt."

Again his aunt reached out and this time ran a hand over his black hair. "You are so like your father," she said. "He was always gentle and always willing to help. You know, he's still with us in a way. As long as you're here, your father's here."

Almost as soon as Dai got up and left, Jerusha came over to Bronwen's work station. "What do you think of the doctor?" she asked immediately.

"Why, I don't know her," Bronwen said with some surprise.

"Well, I don't like her, and I don't trust her."

"What's she done to you?"

"To me? Nothing!" Jerusha exclaimed. "But have you seen what she's done to the captain? There may or may not be wizards on Merlina, but I'll tell you one thing—she's bewitched the captain. He acts like an idiot!"

"She's an attractive woman."

Having already heard this from almost everybody on the ship, Jerusha tossed her head. Her hair bobbed around her face. "What do you feel about her?" She knew that Bronwen too was highly sensitive to what people were like. "Does anything come to you about her? What she's like?"

"Now that you mention it, no. She's very polite, very intelligent . . ." Bronwen became thoughtful. "Now that you mention it," she said again, "I didn't receive any kind of impression at all."

"Neither did I—and neither did Zeno. It's like she's got a wall built around her."

"Well, we all have those, I suppose."

46

"That's what Zeno said, but this is different. Keep your eyes open, Bronwen, and so will I. There's something very wrong about her, and we're going to find out what it is."

"Tell me more about some of your missions, Captain."

"Oh, you can call me Mark."

Dr. Cole looked over her drink at the captain and smiled. She had heavy-lidded eyes, and there was an expression in them that was almost impossible to read. "I'm not sure that would be good for the discipline of the ship."

"I mean when we're alone," Edge said. "And perhaps you wouldn't mind if I call you Temple."

"When we're alone."

Edge leaned forward and began talking again about some of his missions, truthfully elaborating on several of them. Temple Cole's obvious interest was a boost to his ego, and he spoke for some time.

Finally she interrupted, saying, "Mark, we must have more medical supplies."

"Oh, that's easily remedied. I'll take you into the city tomorrow. We can make a day of it."

"That sounds fine." She rose gracefully, saying, "I think I'll turn in, if you don't mind. I'm rather tired, and we have a hard day tomorrow."

"Of course. I'll walk you to your cabin."

As they walked along the corridor, Edge said, "Your cabin isn't much. I can find you a better one, perhaps."

"No, this will be fine."

It was dark outside now, and only the watch crew was stirring. There was a slight humming sound as the engines purred. They talked about the mission until they got to her cabin.

The doctor opened the door, which slid back noiselessly. Before she could step inside, Edge suddenly leaned forward and kissed her.

Putting her hand on his chest, she smiled. "Good night, Captain."

"Good night," Edge said. "I'll be seeing you in the morning."

Temple Cole closed the door and stood still for a moment, thinking. And then she said, *"All right!"*

No one had ever accused Sir Richard Irons of being cheap. Everything he had was the best, and now, looking around the room where he sat on a curved lounge beside a very lovely woman, he was satisfied with what he saw. The room was opulent, the walls glowed with gold, and treasures of paintings and sculpture were everywhere. The major color was crimson, but there were deep greens and purples also.

Irons was a commanding figure. His dark brown hair fell to his shoulders. His deep-set brown eyes had a gold tinge, and there was a handsomeness about him that was imposing. He was six feet three and weighed two hundred and ten pounds, hard, trim, and fit.

"Well, my dear," he said, "I think we're on our way to achieving our goal."

Francesca Del Ray, blonde and blue-eyed, turned lazily to face him. "We've come a long way, Richard."

Francesca Del Ray possessed outward beauty, and those who admired physical beauty were often deceived by it, only to discover that deadliness lay under the smooth exterior.

Francesca poured a drink, sipped half of it, then gave it to Irons. "We haven't come as far as we *will* go, have we?"

"No, my dear. Why shoot for anything other than first?"

Francesca studied Irons, and there was a calculating look in her eyes. "Do you really think you can take over the entire galaxy?"

"Do you think I can't?"

"No one ever has."

"There's never been a man like me before. Nor a woman like you." He admired her appearance, but he was not deceived about her nature. He knew that she was as ruthless as he was himself.

Francesca had started to speak when a soft bell sounded, and Irons, with irritation, said, "What is it?"

"Dr. Temple Cole. She says you sent for her, Excellency."

"So I did."

"Who is that?" Francesca demanded. Probably she too was irritated at their privacy's being invaded.

"A woman. A very beautiful woman."

"Oh?" Francesca's eyebrows went up. "Am I not beautiful enough for you?"

"She's not for me. She's for Captain Mark Edge."

Anger leaped into her eyes. "You should have killed him!"

"A little bit difficult now. Commandant Lee has her eye on him. But I'll find a way, and perhaps this woman will serve."

"May I be permitted to stay for the interview?"

"Are you jealous?"

"Of course."

Raising his voice, he said, "Send Dr. Cole in!" He arose when the door opened. "Ah, Dr. Cole. You're prompt."

"Yes, I try to be, Sir Richard." Her eyes went over to Francesca, who had not risen and who said nothing.

"Dr. Cole, may I present the second in command of my forces, Francesca Del Ray."

The two women studied each other, and Irons was amused to see that the dislike was mutual. "Well, Doctor, what is your report?"

"It was just as you thought. I was accepted instantly as surgeon on board the *Daystar*."

"You're certain that no one suspects that you have seen me?"

"I've been very careful."

"Fine. Now, let's plan our strategy. Sit down, Doctor."

Sitting on a curved maroon chair that seemed to have been designed for her, Dr. Cole prepared to listen. Briefly, her eyes moved to Francesca Del Ray. Then she turned her attention back to Irons.

He spoke slowly. "I think our plan to keep Edge and his crew from interfering with what's happening on Merlina will be much simpler with you as our associate." He turned to Francesca, saying, "I'd like to have your opinion on this, my dear."

"Of course. What is the plan?" Francesca asked, her voice cool and her eyes even cooler.

"It's very simple. Edge is a tough man and clever. We can't take him directly, but every man is a weakling where a woman is concerned. My plan, very simply, is for Dr. Cole to make the captain fall in love with her. Then she can influence him as she pleases."

"Not a very original plan. Edge would be a fool not to see through it."

Irons shrugged. "Most men are fools where women are concerned." He turned to the young doctor, who was watching him carefully. "Have you given this considerable thought?"

"Yes. I haven't changed my mind."

"And do you think you can win the captain over with your womanly wiles?"

"I already have. He's been rather easily led."

"Good. Good. Well, it's settled, then. We've set your fee, and there'll be a large bonus if you succeed. Now, come and let me introduce you to the gentleman who will be your contact here. He will instruct you as to your contact person on Merlina. You'll find the system well in place."

He went to the door and called in a short man with a pair of cold black eyes. "Mr. Conboy, may I introduce your new colleague, Dr. Temple Cole. You will instruct her in our methods."

"Of course, Sir Richard."

Irons watched the two as they started down the hall, then stepped back into the room. "What do you think, my dear?" he asked.

"I'm not convinced she can do it. She's cold."

"Ah, but she has motivation. You see, my dear, she was a physician on a star cruiser for the Intergalactic Council. There was difficulty. She was in love with one of the captains. They came to an impasse, and I won't go into all that. But he blamed it all on her and threw her to the wolves."

"I see. That makes a difference."

"It certainly does. She lost her license to practice medicine, and now she *is* rather 'cold,' as you say. But that needn't enter into the thing. She may, of course, actually fall for Edge and then . . ."

A smile curved her lips. "Such a situation wouldn't bother *me*, Richard. I'm not sure I have a heart to lose."

Irons smiled also. "Neither of us has much in that department, but if we rule the galaxy, we'll learn to get along without hearts."

51

5
Target—Merlina

Edge looked up at Ensign Heck Jordan and tried to keep from smiling. He rarely met anyone who could be more devious than he himself, but it appeared this fifteen-year-old was wise beyond his years, especially when it came to stacking a deck.

Heck had come in and asked to talk with the captain, and Edge had agreed. Now he leaned back in his chair and said, "So, what you're actually suggesting is that we ignore the commandant's direct order. Is that right, Ensign?"

"Well—" Heck shrugged elaborately "—I wouldn't put it exactly that way."

"How exactly would you put it, then?"

"Well . . . it's a long way to Merlina. Everyone knows *that*. So what I would suggest is that we take a shortcut and sort of accidentally bump into Makon."

This time Captain Edge laughed aloud. His white teeth gleamed against his tanned face. "How would you account for the fact that Merlina's in one direction and Makon is in a totally different direction? You don't just *bump into* Makon on your way to Merlina. You have to go there on purpose."

"Why, Captain. I think that could be arranged," Heck said confidentially. "Why don't we just manage to have a navigational failure?"

"That's not likely with a navigator like Bronwen Llewellen. After all, she's probably the most famous navigator alive."

"Oh, sure. Sure. That's the way it was once, but she's getting on in years, you know. I could adjust her instruments. Throw her off just a little, you know. That's after we're underway, of course. Then, when we get lost, we could arrange it so that we wander around for a while and then accidentally wind up on Makon."

"You are some kind of character, Heck! You're worse than I was at your age, and that's saying a lot."

"Why? What have I said that was wrong?" Heck tried to look hurt and failed. He was in the standard uniform adopted by the ensigns but in addition had managed to find a colorful scarf to go around his neck. The scarf utterly clashed with the uniform. It was a repellent, sickly green, but Heck, being color-blind, did not know that. Now he tugged at it. "I don't see anything wrong with wanting to make a little cash."

"Neither do I." Edge frowned. "But I've tried every argument I can think of on Commandant Lee, and she's flatly refused. So it's out of the question."

Heck sighed deeply, then spread his hands in a helpless gesture. "Well, Captain, I think you and I can work on this. I'm not giving up. After all, a man owes it to himself to do the best he can."

"Right. Even if it means disobeying a direct order of the commandant of the Intergalactic Council?"

Heck squirmed uncomfortably. "Well, you and I, we're alike on this. Women, they don't seem to understand that a man has to do whatever he has to do to get ahead. Right, Captain?"

"I used to think so," Edge said softly, "but now I don't have any choice. We're on our way to Merlina, and that's it."

Much faster than Mark Edge had reckoned, all of

the thousand and one details involved in getting a space cruiser on its way were accomplished.

"How do the boards look, Jerusha?"

"We've got green lights systemwide except for engine intermix. We should be seeing a green light for that in five minutes."

"What's shield strength?" Edge asked, going down his list.

"Shield's up to seventy-six per cent strength. When the intermix normalizes, the shields will be very close to one hundred percent."

"Edge to Navigations."

"Llewellen here, Captain."

"Have you finished plotting the course to Merlina?"

"Plotted and laid in. Navigation computer shows green, Captain. We're ready to go."

"Edge to Jaleel."

"Here, sir," answered the weapons officer.

"Status on turbo cannons."

"The pulse repeaters are a little slow. Ensign Ericson and I will work on them once we are under way."

"Edge to Engineering."

"I wondered when you were going to get to me," Ivan said.

"Never mind the sarcasm, Lieutenant. Engine status?"

Ivan drew the communicator up to his lips and reported, "The engine intermix is almost complete. The engineering computers are five by five." Ivan liked using the old terms that meant things were all right.

Finally all was ready, and Edge sat back in the seat before his console. "Ready for liftoff, Commander Thrax."

"Yes sir. Everything is in order," Thrax said easily.

This *Daystar* handled a lot more smoothly than its predecessor. The thruster assemblies lifted the ship five hundred meters in seconds. The forward stabilizers now had room to extend to full length. The engines then fired, and *Daystar* shot forward majestically, turning its nose upward toward the ionosphere. The old *Daystar* shook like a tin can in the atmosphere. This new *Daystar* was as smooth as silk. Captain Edge had christened her the *Daystar 831-B*.

They raced upward, and the blue sky became lighter in color until it turned clear. In front of them lay the vast, star-specked blackness of outer space.

Once the ship was clear of Earth's atmosphere, and Bronwen Llewellen had set the course, Edge relaxed. He left the bridge and went to find Mei-Lani.

She was in the observatory and got up quickly as he entered. "A wonderful takeoff, Captain."

"Thanks, Mei-Lani." Edge sat down. "Now, tell me everything you know about Merlina."

"Yes sir!"

"Well, sit. You don't have to stand at attention. Just be at ease."

"Yes, Captain." Mei-Lani sat and thought for a moment, then began. "As you may know, Captain, there was once a series of myths about a man called King Arthur. Historians were never sure whether there had been a real King Arthur or not. It was more likely," she added, "that there had been a minor tribal chieftain who did rather wonderful deeds. Later on, after his death, legends began to collect about him."

"I've heard of that. What does that have to do with Merlina?"

"Well, part of the legend of Arthur is tied in with a magician—a sorcerer—named Merlin. He was a very powerful man in the arts of magic, so the fables go. Of course, in those days magicians were more or less highly respected. They were even feared for their supernatural powers, and it seems Merlin had some of those. At least according to the legend."

Edge listened as Mei-Lani described how the planet was settled by a certain group of colonists.

"They were unhappy with things on Earth. During that period of time, magicians were out of favor. The church was strong and totally opposed to what they called black magic. This group was into the occult, the worship of demons and the Devil—even practiced human sacrifice."

"That's pretty grim. Is there any of that around today, Mei-Lani?"

"I'm afraid so, Captain. But not so much as we will be likely to find on Merlina. Anyway, these people landed there and have based their whole culture on demon worship."

"I understand they don't have powerful modern weapons, though, like our Neuromags."

"No. Not that kind of weapon. Not the kind you're thinking of."

Mei-Lani described some of the activities of the wizards of Merlina. "The wizards took that name for themselves, so the information I have goes. But you must not underestimate them, Captain."

"Well, they can't stand up against our turbo cannons and Neuromags," Edge said confidently.

"Don't be too sure of that. The question is whether or not we'll be able to stand up against *their* powers. It would be a serious error to underestimate them."

"I don't believe in witches and things like that, Mei-Lani."

"I know that, Captain," she said softly, "but there *are* powerful dark forces in this galaxy. It all began when the Devil was separated from God. According to the Bible, it appears he was once the highest angel, but he grew proud and rebelled against God. Then there was war in heaven, and since that time the universe has been contaminated with evil."

Edge had listened to all this rather casually. "I think we can handle it, Mei-Lani, but thanks for your information. If you put this into a report, I'd like to have a copy of it and anything else you can think of that might help us."

"Yes sir. I'd be glad to."

Traveling through space was not like anything else, Mark Edge thought. It was a different kind of travel altogether. It was hard to "wish upon a star" when you were racing by them at many times the speed of light.

"Don't you think the star field is just beautiful, Captain?" Raina asked, studying the forward viewer.

"To tell you the truth, Ensign St. Clair, it would make me happier if we were looking at the star clusters that surround Makon. I think this trip is a waste of my valuable time."

The crew settled in and fell into a working routine. All seemed to be going well except, as Jerusha repeatedly pointed out at the beginning, the captain had his mind on things beside operating a star cruiser.

Day after day went by, and she kept close watch on the captain's activities with Dr. Temple Cole. She'd stopped talking to others about her concerns, but one day she felt she had to do something. She went to the captain's cabin.

"Hello, Ensign Ericson," Edge said cheerfully.

"Captain, I need to talk to you."

"Something wrong?"

Jerusha hesitated. "I think so. You may not like what I have to say."

"Well, why don't you tell me what it is, and I'll decide whether I like it, Jerusha. Sit down. Will you have something to drink? Maybe a snack?"

"No sir. I think not." Jerusha had tried to decide how to put this in a way that would not offend the captain. Nevertheless, now that the time had come, she knew that complete honesty was the only way to go.

"I'm concerned about Dr. Cole," she said bluntly.

"What about Dr. Cole? She's a competent surgeon."

"Well, sir, we don't even know that. She hasn't actually done anything yet, but there's something wrong with her."

"What do you mean, *wrong?*" Edge's tone was as sharp as his name, and he straightened his back, a scowl on his face. "Do you have some charges to make?"

Jerusha swallowed hard. "No sir. Nothing that I can prove, but I will tell you this. She's hiding something. I don't know what it is, but it's not natural for anyone to be as . . . well, as *closed* as she is."

"Oh, you're having trouble picking up on her emotions."

"That's it." Then she blurted out, "I see *you're* not having any trouble picking up on her emotions," and knew immediately that she had made a mistake.

Edge stood to his feet. "Interview is over, Ensign!"

"But, Captain—"

"I said the interview is over!"

"Yes sir."

Jerusha left the cabin, her face flaming. "I didn't handle that too well," she muttered as she went down the passageway. "Well, I don't care what he says! There *is* something wrong!"

Two days after Jerusha's meeting with the captain, one of the crewmen, a middle-aged man named Simms, was badly injured when a piece of the superstructure that he was repairing collapsed. He was rushed to the sick bay, where Dr. Cole at once took over. Everyone knew that the injury was serious, and Jerusha, especially, waited anxiously to see how the doctor handled it.

She found out when Edge came out and said, "Well, Jerusha, you'll be glad to know we have a competent surgeon. Simms is doing fine. He's going to live and be as good as ever, thanks to the competent care of Dr. Temple Cole."

"I'm happy to hear it, sir. Simms is a good man."

"You didn't expect it, though, did you?"

"Sir, I really never doubted Dr. Cole's medical ability. I don't know anything about that, but it seems she is very able. That's not what troubles me about her."

Edge stared at her. "Jerusha, I think you're depending on your impressions too much. I know you're a highly sensitive person, but you're not infallible. I've found the doctor not only to be a competent physician but an amiable young woman, well suited for star cruiser duty. I would appreciate it if you would not mention this matter again!"

For a week, Jerusha continued to carry out her duties, seeing the captain and the surgeon grow closer daily. There was still nothing that she could put her finger on, nothing she could put in a report to make a complaint. Besides, who was there to complain to? There was the captain, and she had already complained to him.

One afternoon she was in the lounge alone when Dr. Cole came in.

The doctor said, "Do you mind if I sit down?"

"Please do," Jerusha said. As the surgeon took a seat, again Jerusha tried to understand her, to sense something—anger, hostility, anything—but no impression came.

Without preliminaries, Dr. Cole looked across the table and said, "Well, Ensign, it appears that you don't like me."

"That's right. I don't," Jerusha replied.

"I'm sorry for that. Have I done anything to offend you?"

"No, you have not."

"I understand you're exceptionally astute. Perhaps you've been picking up some bad vibes from me."

Jerusha shook her head. "On the contrary, Dr. Cole. I haven't picked up anything at all. You're a very difficult woman to read. The most difficult I've ever been around."

"So you haven't read my mind?" She smiled.

"Not I. First Officer Thrax is the one accused of mind reading. But I must tell you that he says he finds you difficult also."

"Why are you so interested in what I'm like?"

"Because I'm interested in this ship and in—"

"And in Captain Edge."

Jerusha felt herself flushing. "Of course, I'm interested. He's my captain."

Again Temple Cole smiled. Her violet eyes surveyed the girl across from her, and she was silent for a moment. Then she said, "When I was your age, Jerusha, I became terribly infatuated with a doctor. It was awful. He was in his late twenties, and I was only fifteen, but to me it was the most serious thing in the world. As I look back on it now, I see that the experience wasn't nearly as life threatening as I thought it was at the time. I came, finally, to understand it for what it was—just a girlish infatuation."

She stood to her feet. "You'll outgrow it, Jerusha. I'm sorry you don't like me. But, really, I think you're only experiencing a bad case of juvenile jealousy."

Jerusha sat there furious, anger raging through her as the doctor left. She gritted her teeth and muttered to herself, "It's not juvenile jealousy, Dr. Temple Cole—and you are *not* what you pretend to be!"

She got up and tried to regain her composure. "We've got a long trip, and somewhere along the way I'll find out what it is that you're hiding behind that wall!"

6

Love Isn't Logical

The days stretched on, and as the *Daystar* flashed through the heavens, threading her way past untold stars that twinkled like miniature diamonds, Captain Edge practically left the running of the ship to his first officer.

Mark Edge was not entirely ignorant where women were concerned. His rough good looks and brash smile had brought him to the attention of many. But never had he fallen for anyone as he had for his new surgeon. Ever since Temple Cole had first come aboard the *Daystar*, he had been charmed by her in a way that he could not explain.

It became his custom to entertain the doctor every evening in his cabin. This evening had been especially satisfying, Edge thought.

He had requested Jerusha to prepare a particularly fine private dinner, telling her, "It's my birthday, and I'm celebrating."

Jerusha had glanced at him sharply, but she agreed without comment and went off—presumably to ask Mei-Lani and Raina to arrange something special for the captain.

The lights in the captain's cabin were turned down low, and most of the illumination came from the candelabra, which held six crimson candles that made yellow dots of flame. The mellow light that they cast highlighted Temple Cole's regular features, and the semi-darkness made her large eyes appear even larger.

"Happy birthday, Captain," she said, raising her crystal goblet.

"Thank you, Temple. When is *your* birthday?"

"I've stopped counting them," she said. She sipped her drink and smiled. "A woman has to stop having birthdays after a certain age."

"You don't have to worry about that." His eyes were filled with admiration. The doctor had dressed for the occasion. She wore a gold lamé tunic with a full maroon skirt. Her hair was done in a new way, with curls piled on top of her head.

"You're always complimentary, Mark," she murmured. "I've enjoyed the voyage very much."

Edge rose and said, "Let's go watch the stars out the port."

She walked with him to the round porthole that looked out into the infinity of space. "The stars are much more beautiful in space. You can see the colors. It looks almost like a huge decoration out here, spangled and glowing," she murmured.

The evening went on, and finally Temple said, "It's time for me to go."

"Stay a while longer," he urged.

"No. That would make talk. It's getting late. I'll see you in the morning."

Dr. Cole walked down the corridor to her cabin. Sitting before her mirror, she removed her coral earrings, then began taking down her hair. As she did so, she looked at herself in the glass, and it was like looking at a stranger.

Her thoughts screamed at her, *I'm hurting this man. He trusts me and seems to care for me, and I'm setting out to ruin him.*

Disturbed by her guilty conscience, she prepared

for bed. But sleep eluded her. The disciplined Temple Cole was surprised to find her conscience highly active. She could not forget the look on Mark Edge's face. Her thoughts went to Sir Richard Irons, and she contrasted the two men. Both were strong men, but Irons was without mercy. Captain Edge had some other qualities.

"Still, why should I be kind after what was done to me?" she said aloud. "Edge himself is no better than a pirate, taking what he wants."

But this did not soothe her conscience, and she thought bitterly, *I know how to shut away my thoughts from others, but I can't shut them away from myself.*

Before breakfast the next morning the soft bell that signaled a visitor rang in Temple Cole's cabin. Surprised, she straightened her tunic and said, "Enter."

When the door slid back, she was surprised to see Zeno Thrax, the first officer. "Why, yes. What is it, First?"

"I wonder if I might speak to you, Dr. Cole."

"Certainly. Come in—or would you rather go to the medical station?"

"No. This isn't a medical problem."

"Oh! Well, come in then. Will you have a seat?"

Thrax remained standing, and his colorless eyes were intense as he fixed them on her.

"Why did you come, Commander?" the doctor asked. There was something about the albino's unblinking stare that made her nervous. Besides, she had not slept well and was edgy. "If you want to see me about a problem, perhaps we'd better go to the medical center after all."

"I think *you* have a problem, Dr. Cole."

A start of fear went through her. "And what do you mean by that? Have you been reading my mind?"

"No. That I can't do." Thrax put his hands behind his back and tilted his head to one side. "But I sense you have perfected a block. You won't let yourself be known by *anyone*. That could mean that you're hiding something, Dr. Cole."

"Isn't everyone?" There was a slight bitterness in her tone. "What are *you* hiding, Zeno?"

Zeno looked down. The silence seemed to swell in the room, until finally he said, "I betrayed my people, and I can never go home."

The simple confession touched something in Temple Cole. For one fleeting moment she had the fervent wish that she could confess *her* wrongdoing as simply as this man had done. But all she could do was say, "I'm so sorry, Zeno!"

Zeno looked up, pain in his pale eyes. "To my sorrow, I know something about betrayal. Betrayal doesn't destroy the one it is directed against so much as the one who is guilty. When we hurt others, we really hurt ourselves."

"Did you come here to deliver a sermon? And who is it you think I'm betraying?" the surgeon demanded. "And what's your evidence?"

"I have no evidence, Doctor. It's just that it's unusual for anyone to close himself off as much as you do."

"There's nothing wrong with me, and until you have evidence to the contrary, I suggest you not make accusations."

Zeno stared at her briefly, then nodded. "I'm sorry to have disturbed you."

He retreated through the door, and Temple Cole felt a wave of relief as it closed behind him. The confrontation had shaken her, and her emotions raged. Once she had been a woman who had good qualities, but her betrayal by a man she loved and trusted had left its mark on her. She said aloud, "I can't give up. This is my only chance to get what I want."

A voice seemed to whisper, "What *do* you want, Temple?"

As if another person had asked the question, she said, "I want enough money so that I'll never have to put myself in anyone's hands again! And I can get it from Richard Irons. After that—"

She did not finish, but her eyes narrowed, and her lips grew thin. "I'm going to have what I want." She moved toward the door, her mind made up.

"That's a bad cut, Ensign St. Clair. How did you get it?"

Temple had managed to bury her guilty conscience, and by the time Raina St. Clair came into the sick bay with her hand wrapped with a cloth, she was in command of herself. She examined the deep cut and listened to Raina explain how she had been working with Ivan Petroski on the communications system when a screwdriver had slipped and gouged her palm.

"That'll have to have a few stitches. Here, I'll put it to sleep." Reaching into a cabinet, Dr. Cole pulled out what looked like a flashlight. She aimed it at the injured palm. When she threw a switch, a greenish light shot out, and Raina's hand seemed to glow. "Is that all right?"

"Yes. I can't feel a thing."

Putting the sonolight back into its case, the surgeon remarked, "Back in the old days, it wasn't as easy. Doctors had to stick needles into people, and before that time there was practically nothing to take away pain."

"I know. Mei-Lani was telling me that when they

had to amputate limbs during the American Civil War, all they could do was give the soldiers a piece of lead to bite on." She shuddered. "It must've been awful."

"We have come a long way indeed, but there's more to do yet."

"Where did you get your medical training, Dr. Cole?" Raina asked as the doctor sterilized the wound and her own hands and then began to stitch up the gaping cut.

The doctor explained where she had gone to school.

Then Raina asked, "You're not married?"

Something behind Dr. Cole's eyes closed as if a curtain had come down.

"No. I never married."

"I'm sorry. I didn't mean to be personal." She watched as the doctor skillfully put in the stitches. As Dr. Cole was bandaging the hand, Raina said, "I've been hoping you'd come to one of our services, Dr. Cole."

"I have no time for that, I'm afraid."

"You're not a Christian, then?"

Temple Cole eyed the girl. She had always been impressed by Raina St. Clair's physical attractiveness, but her religious interest was something else. "I don't believe in such things. I can only believe what I see, what can be explained by scientific fact. And I don't see how a man dying thousands of years ago could do anything for me. It's not logical."

"Well, many real things aren't logical, Doctor."

"I'm a scientist. I believe in facts."

Raina looked thoughtful. "Haven't you ever encountered anything that couldn't be explained?"

"No."

Something flared in Raina's eyes. "Dr. Cole, I was in a fire when I was just a child. There was no hope for me, but my father came bursting in. He managed to carry me out, but he died from his burns. Was that logical to give his life for his child? No, it wasn't, and for Jesus to die for sinners is not logical. But love isn't *logical*, Doctor."

Dr. Cole had heard such things before, but as the girl went on to explain how Jesus loved sinners, something tugged at her heart. It was a pulling, a drawing, and a longing rose in her to know more about this man who, it was said, could forgive sins. But then she repeated, "I have no time for that."

"Come to the service, will you, Doctor?"

"I won't be there."

Later that evening when Temple Cole was having dinner with the captain, she was still disturbed. All day long she'd seemed to hear Raina St. Clair say, "Love isn't logical." What was happening inside her was unlike anything she had ever felt before.

Later still, the captain reached across and put his hand over hers. "I'm falling in love with you, Temple."

But Dr. Cole suddenly thought of the other man that she had loved. Yet he had betrayed her. She looked up and said quietly, "No, I'm afraid you're just playing games. All men do that."

"This isn't a game," Captain Edge protested. "I wish you could believe that."

Temple Cole lowered her eyes, and she thought, *I can't believe anything anymore. I don't know what's happening to me!*

7

Out of the Depths

Commander Zeno, I want to keep our presence a secret from the wizards as long as possible."

Thrax nodded. "Yes sir. I believe that will be possible." He turned to the communications officer. "Raina, help me plot a landing area close to this city." On the chart, he pointed to the largest city on the planet.

Glancing at Thrax, Raina whispered, "I don't think this will work. The wizards are the servants of Satan. They knew about us as soon as we entered this sector."

But First never looked away from the planetary chart that the navigational computer had brought up. Pointing to a position northwest of the city, he said, "I think that's the spot. It gives us good cover in a forest."

Raina studied her console. "I agree there are no signals coming from that location. It appears pretty quiet."

The captain swung *Daystar* into a wide, low arc until she was less than fifty meters from the ground. He was an excellent pilot. Raina knew that everyone else aboard was a nervous wreck. Flying a spaceship this close to the ground at this speed was suicidal. But Edge grinned from ear to ear. He loved to show off his flying skills.

When *Daystar* approached the landing coordinates, the captain threw the forward thrusters on full, stopping the ship at the exact spot Thrax had shown him.

As the small cruiser descended to the ground, Heck and Ringo picked themselves up off the floor.

Jerusha, who had secured her seat belt, looked down at the two ruffled ensigns. With frustration in her voice she said, "How many times is this going to happen to you? If I've told you once, I've told you a million times, *fasten your seat belt!*"

Heck looked back at her and shrugged his shoulders.

When the ship came to a halt, Captain Edge barked, "All right! Prepare for a scouting party!"

Mei-Lani said, "Captain, I feel I must warn you. The dangers that the scouting party will face will not be so much physical as spiritual."

"Now, Mei-Lani, we've been over that before." Exasperation and impatience sounded in Edge's voice. "We can handle anything that they can throw at us."

"Captain, shall I lead the landing party?" Lieutenant Jaleel's eyes flashed with excitement.

"I'll be leading the party, but you're welcome to accompany us, Lieutenant."

The scouting party, when it assembled outside the *Daystar*, was armed with Neuromag sidearms, all set on the "stun" phase.

"We don't want to harm any of the inhabitants. That's not our purpose here," Edge said. He looked over their equipment. "Well, I think we're ready to go."

Besides Captain Edge and Jaleel, the group included Dai Bando, Dr. Cole, and Raina St. Clair.

Ringo, Heck, and Jerusha stood watching the scouting party move out into the thickly foliaged countryside.

"That's dumb," Jerusha said.

"What's dumb?" Heck was eating a cookie, his eyes half closed with pleasure.

Heck got more pleasure from eating, Ringo thought,

than anybody he had ever seen. He watched him pop the last morsel into his mouth and start on another.

"Taking Dr. Cole on a scouting party," Jerusha said. "He should have taken me!"

Heck reached over and gave Jerusha a hug. "He just don't appreciate you like I do, baby. Give up on him, and turn your attention on a real man."

"Get your hands off of me, Heck!" Jerusha exploded. She tore herself free from his grasp and stalked off.

"Well, what's eating her, do you suppose?" Heck said with surprise, taking another bite of cookie.

Ringo watched Jerusha disappear. He pretty well knew the situation, but he would say nothing about it. *She's got a heavy crush on Captain Edge, and I wish she didn't.* He knew something about crushes, having one himself on Raina St. Clair, about which he would also say nothing. He looked out the porthole at the scouting party as they disappeared into the trees and said, "I wish I could go with them."

"I think we've been by this big tree before."

Dai Bando stood looking up at a strange, twisted tree. Its trunk spiraled, and it had no branches until they suddenly sprang out some forty feet above the ground. "I never saw a tree like this, and I think we came by here a few hours ago."

"That can't be," Captain Edge growled.

"I think the ensign is right, Captain," Lieutenant Jaleel said. "See." She pointed down at the ground, which was still soft from the rain that had drenched them all.

Edge walked over and looked down at footprints. "Are these ours?"

"I think they are," Jaleel said. "We're going around in circles."

73

"Well, no wonder. This is a trackless place with nothing to mark your position." Edge looked at his compass and scowled. "We're going in the right direction, but somehow we've gone in a circle. How's that possible?"

Raina said, "I don't know about the compass, but I remember Mei-Lani once telling me that most people have one leg shorter than the other. When they're in a place like this and have no guides, they go a little bit, just a fraction, in the direction of the short leg."

"I believe that's true," Temple Colc said. She was flushed, and her legs were trembling. The others were in good physical condition, having been trained for some time for missions like this, but she had not. She wanted desperately to sit and rest but did not dare say so.

"We should be able to trust our compass! Well, let's go on for another hour or two. It'll be getting dark soon, and I don't want to be caught without some kind of shelter," Captain Edge replied.

Dr. Cole stumbled on, trying not to show her fatigue.

Dai Bando came up beside her. "If you're tired, I can carry you."

Astonished, she looked at him. "Carry me?" She gasped. "That's impossible."

"Oh, no. If it wouldn't embarrass you."

By this time Temple was past being embarrassed. The others were far ahead, and she took a deep breath. "I can't keep up, Dai. Can you really carry me?"

"Ho!" He laughed, his white teeth flashing against his darkly tanned skin. "Nothing easier." He squatted down. "Just get on my shoulders, Doctor."

Cautiously Temple Cole did as the boy suggested. When she was astride, he suddenly rose, and she grabbed wildly at him, holding onto his forehead.

74

He laughed again and said, "Here we go!"

He began a gait that was easy and smooth. He was almost running with her weight on his shoulders, and he seemed not to be conscious of it. "Are you all right up there, Doctor?"

Dr. Cole was holding onto his curly hair. "I'm fine, Dai, but aren't I too heavy?"

"Not a bit. I'm going to speed up." He broke into a run, and she began to feel exhilaration as she rode along, holding on. The faster pace somehow made it easier for her. Soon they caught up with the others, who turned and looked. She laughed at the surprised expression on Mark Edge's face, and when they drew closer, she said, "I had to ask Dai to give me a ride."

Edge grinned. "I wish I'd thought of it first. I'm getting pretty tired myself." He looked around and then pointed over to his left. "Over there. We'll camp for the night under those big trees. Break out the supplies."

The group gathered beneath the trees.

Dai stooped down again, and Dr. Cole slipped off. She put out her hand, and when he took it, she smiled at him. "Thanks for the ride, Dai."

"Any time, Doctor."

"You're very strong."

Dai simply shrugged. Then he said, "Captain, would you like for me to recon the perimeter?"

"Yes, Ensign, that would be good."

As Dai went loping off, Dr. Cole said, "That's a remarkable young man. I've never seen anyone so strong."

"Yes, he is, and he's fast too. Isn't he, Lieutenant Jaleel?"

Edge said this slyly, and displeasure flared in the lieutenant's eyes. "Well, Lieutenant, let's unpack the cooking gear. Then we'll see if we can cook up something. A hot meal wouldn't be bad."

As the rations were heating on the portable stove, Dai Bando reported to the captain. "The perimeter is secure, Captain. I'll check it once an hour."

Edge looked down at the bland-looking food and said, "Dai, I'm going to circle the perimeter once myself. If I'm lucky, I'll get us some fresh meat. Meantime, you build us a nice campfire." Edge walked away, readjusting his Neuromag setting to "kill."

The campfire burned steadily, sending up tongues of red and yellow flame, and the crackling of the dry wood made a pleasant sound. All of the party was seated around it, eating the last of the game that they had roasted over the fire. Captain Edge had shot a deerlike animal, and they had enjoyed the tasty flavor of the meat along with the fresh water that Dai found in a brook nearby.

"Well, that was a good meal," Edge commented. He was sitting cross-legged, staring into the fire, apparently hypnotized by the leaping flames.

Dai continued to nibble at his meat, pulling pieces of it from the bone. Then he said, "I think I'll get some sleep. I'm tired." He moved away from the fire, rolled up in a blanket, and seemed to fall asleep instantly.

Lieutenant Jaleel stared at him. "He must have a good conscience." She went off to roll up in her own blanket.

For a short time Raina sat listening to Mark Edge talk about the mission. She studied the faces of the captain and Dr. Cole and felt a longing to see them change. The captain was a decent man, she knew, though not a Christian. As for Dr. Cole, Raina was convinced there was something in her heart that the surgeon could not bear to talk about.

At last Raina said, "I think I'll turn in too. I'm very tired."

Edge responded. "That would be a good idea, Raina. It might be a rough day tomorrow."

"I always did hate to go to bed," Edge said.

"You weren't afraid of the dark, were you, Mark?"

"No, I was always afraid I'd miss something."

Temple Cole looked out beyond their sleeping companions into the darkness of the junglelike foliage that surrounded them. "You're not likely to miss anything out here unless some beast comes along to liven things up."

Edge laughed. "You have a way of putting things, Temple. Now I'll stay awake thinking about a lion or something jumping on me."

They sat by the fire for a long time, and at last Temple asked, "What was your life like when you were growing up? I'd like to have known you when you were a little boy."

"I wasn't a great deal of fun, Temple," he said after a silence.

"What about your parents?"

"I really didn't know them. They both died before I was six. I lived with relatives for a while, and then I went to the Space Academy. Got kicked out for conduct unbecoming a space cadet." He grinned. "Want to know the circumstances?"

Temple smiled back. She hugged her knees and said, "I bet it wasn't anything simple."

"You're wrong there. It was simple. I smuggled a young lady aboard a ship, got caught, and got shucked out."

"Well, that was simple enough," she agreed. "What did you do then?"

"I became a gentleman adventurer." Edge reached over and picked up a stick. He poked at the logs until they shifted. There was a hissing sound, and sparks went upward, swarming around in miniature whirls that disappeared in the treetops. He turned to her with another grin. "Roughly translated, that means I became a pirate."

"Not really!"

"More or less. It was a rough way to grow up. I worked for Sir Richard Irons for a while. He took me on as one of his captains. You can't get more like a pirate than Irons, and he expects no less from those who serve under him."

"What's he like?" Temple knew very well what Sir Richard Irons was like, but she did not know exactly what Captain Edge was like. She listened as he described Irons much as she herself had seen him—a man with a smooth manner but no more mercy than a snake.

As Edge talked on about his past, his struggles, she felt something stir within herself. *This is the man I'm betraying. He's worked so hard, and I'm going to deliver him into the hands of the wizards of Merlina. They'll hand him over to Sir Richard Irons, and I know what will happen then.*

She had heard the story of the tridium, the diamondlike substance on Makon, and knew that Sir Richard Irons would stop short of nothing, not even torture, to get the secret of the planet's location from Edge. Her conscience suddenly became very active.

Abruptly she said, "Good night, Mark. It's late."

"Good night, Temple."

She went to roll up in her blanket and tried to sleep, but for a long time she lay there, secretly watching the tall man as he nursed the fire. The dying firelight illuminated his face, and she could see the strength that was there. He was not a perfect man, she well knew that, but he was basically honorable.

And Dr. Temple Cole was not.

Dawn seemed to come at a single leap. One moment it was dark, and the next the sun was sending yellow streamers through the trees and the brambles into the small open place where they had made camp.

They breakfasted on leftover cold meat and what few supplies they had, and then Edge said, "It's time to move on."

"You need another ride, Doctor?" Dai approached, smiling at Temple Cole.

"Not yet. I'm pretty sore, but I can make it for a while."

"Anytime. It's no trouble."

"Thank you, Dai."

The party soon left the jungle for a clearer region, much like a plain. As they started through it, Jaleel warned them, "Be careful! I don't like walking around with our weapons on stun. What if something really bad came at us?"

Edge shook his head. "And I don't want to take the chance of killing any of the inhabitants here. I made some bad mistakes on Makon, and I don't want to repeat them. We've got to contact some of these people and find out what's going on."

"Suppose we contact the wrong ones?" Raina asked. "From what I understand, the wizards control the planet, and they've subdued the Merlinians."

"We'll just have to be careful." He frowned. "I suppose we should have brought Jerusha with us. If we did encounter any of the inhabitants, she'd be handy for telling us something about what they were like. On the inside, I mean."

"It's too late for that now," Raina said dryly, "but I wish she were here, too."

They threaded their way across a broken field. Huge rocks pushed up from the crust of the earth, and dark holes appeared here and there.

Dai Bando peered down into one of them and then shivered. "I don't like holes in the ground," he muttered. "Look down there. You can't even see the bottom of it."

"Come away from that hole, Dai!" Dr. Cole said quickly. She took his arm to pull him away. Then she too glanced down. "That doesn't look good to me, either. I wonder what could have made a crater like that?"

"Just stay away from them!" Tara Jaleel said. "If you fell down one of those things, I doubt if we'd have enough rope to get you out."

They continued to encounter the deep holes, and the land became even more broken. It was altogether unlike the thickly foliaged area where they had landed.

At midday they stopped for a lunch break. As they ate some dried food and drank water from their canteens, Edge said, "I don't see that we're doing any good. We're going in a straight line, apparently, but we haven't seen a living soul. There must be somebody around."

"We probably just landed in an uninhabitable place," Dr. Cole said. She looked about at the barrenness. "Maybe we ought to go back to the ship and circle until we see the city."

"I don't want to be seen if I can help it," Edge said. "We'll go on for another couple of hours. Then, if we don't find any towns or any people, we'll turn back."

Then he ordered them to spread out so that they could cover more territory.

After an hour, Temple was exhausted again. Her muscles were sore from the strenuous effort the day before, but she gritted her teeth and kept going. She glanced over to her left and saw Tara Jaleel slogging forward, but she was only a small figure in the distance. Over to her right she looked for Mark Edge, but he was invisible.

Despite her protesting muscles, she stumbled on. Again she saw one of the dark, noisome holes that they still encountered from time to time. These had become so common, however, that she did not pay any attention.

She had passed by the crater when a slight noise attracted her attention. Whirling around, she was horrified to see something coming out of the hole, and that something was the most horrible thing she had ever seen.

Out of the pit slithered a nightmarish creature! It was serpentlike, but it was more than a serpent. It had two scaly arms extending from a head that appeared to be all teeth. A pair of brilliant yellow eyes glowed as they fastened themselves on her. And then, as the huge creature further emerged, she saw that it was heavily scaled. The scales rustled and rattled as it slithered across the ground. The body was fully a foot and a half in diameter. The head was even larger, and now the beast cleared the hole and sat coiled before her.

Temple had never known such fear as came over her. She fumbled for the Neuromag on her belt. The coiled serpent rose up, its head and neck back in striking position, as she had seen rattlesnakes do.

Temple Cole knew that a sidearm set on stun would never stop this monster. Finding her voice, she screamed, whirled, and began to run. Behind her, she could hear the slithering of scales, and when she looked back she saw that the awful thing was gaining on her. She ran as fast as she could, but the sound kept coming closer. And then she stumbled and fell headlong.

Rolling to one side, she saw the creature's mouth open so that its black maw was visible, and the long, sharp teeth fairly glinted. She screamed again, "No! No!"

The serpent lunged forward—and then suddenly, from nowhere, a figure hurled itself onto the reptile's scaly back.

Mark Edge threw himself on the serpent, wrapping his legs around the thickened body, holding it just under the head. He had not taken time to reset his Neuromag but gripped the dagger that he always wore at his side. He began slashing at the monster and discovered, to his horror, that the creature's scales turned the blade. He was dimly aware that Temple Cole was on her feet, watching.

"Run!" he shouted.

The beast hissed horribly and began thrashing about. Obviously the creature was intelligent, for it reared upward and then backward, smashing him against the rocks.

The captain grunted with pain. The muscular body of the monster writhed and rolled beneath his grip, and he knew he could not hold on long. He made a wild slash and struck the creature's eye. It went dull instantly, but a scream of rage burst from the reptile's throat.

Over and over the serpent writhed, banging him against the sharp projections of rock, cutting and bruising his flesh. He knew if he let go, the saberlike teeth would finish him at once, but his strength was ebbing, and the blows that he took were weakening him.

Can't take much more of this, he thought and tried again to pierce the armored scales.

The animal reared once more, threw itself backwards, and Mark hit the ground hard. His head struck against an outcropping of rock, and he felt the world swimming around. He scrambled to his knees but could get no farther, for the beast, one eye gleaming and one dead, was coiled before him, ready to strike.

Mark knew he was a dead man, and he experienced what he had heard some people do when about to die. His whole life seemed to flash before him in seconds. He felt bitterness over things left undone—and some things done that would have been better if he had never done them. He thought briefly of the future. *I'll never know now what it's like to live to be an old man—*

The serpent's head went back. Its fierce fangs glittered. Mark saw the death strike begin, and he knew it was over.

And then a beam of red light suddenly appeared. The light ray struck the beast in the head, and instantly the remaining living eye glazed over. The creature flopped to the earth, where it began twisting in death throes. It rolled over several times, then quivered and lay still.

Mark struggled to his feet and turned toward Temple Cole, who was lowering her weapon. She dropped the Neuromag and ran to him. "Mark, are you all right?"

He wasn't all right. He was hurting all over. Blood was streaming from the back of his head where he had been smashed against the rock, and he was bruised and cut, but he stared at her with admiration. "You set your Neuromag for kill. You saved my life, Temple."

"No. You saved *my* life, Mark."

Dizziness began to attack him then. He muttered, "I don't . . . feel too good . . ." He swayed and pitched forward.

Temple caught him as best she could. She cradled his head in her arm and looked down at his unconscious face. All she could think of was *I came here to betray him, and he risked his life with that monstrous beast to save me.* Tears ran unheeded down her cheeks.

She was still sitting there when the others came running up. Jaleel looked at the dead serpent and flinched. "So that's what's in those holes. Did the captain kill it?"

But Temple Cole merely shook her head. "We've got to take care of him. Make camp, and I'll see what I can do. He's been pretty badly hurt."

Dai Bando scooped up the captain and trotted effortlessly away toward a copse of trees, saying, "Come on. This looks like a good spot over here."

Raina helped Temple Cole to her feet. She studied the face of the older woman. "I believe God was with you, wasn't He?"

"Yes," she whispered, "He was!"

Temple Cole, for the first time in her life, had admitted that there was such a being as God.

8

A Sudden Encounter

Dr. Cole treated the captain as well as she could, but she said aside to Dai Bando, "He was badly banged up. I'm glad he didn't get bitten. No telling what sort of poison might have been in the fangs of that horrid creature."

"I wonder if we ought to turn back," Dai pondered. "Do you think he's able to go on?"

"I talked to him about it, but you know he's a stubborn man."

Dai grinned suddenly. "Yes, he is. If he says he's going on, he'll go even if I have to carry him."

They rested for one day, and at the third dawn Captain Edge stretched cautiously. "Well," he said with relief, "I'm pretty sore, but no reason for turning back."

"Are you sure, Captain?" Temple asked anxiously. "You took a terrible beating from that creature."

"I've had worse. No, we'll go on."

Despite the surgeon's protest, Captain Edge would not hear of stopping. They moved on across the badlands all morning, and at about noon Jaleel said, "Look ahead. I think we're coming into a different kind of country."

"That suits me," Dai said. "I don't like this country anyway."

They walked all afternoon, passing out of the rough country onto a plain that was broken occasionally by copses of trees. The Merlina sun had been hot, and as it slowly went down, Temple took a deep breath. "It's going to get cooler tonight, surely." Looking over at the captain, she added, "And you've gone far enough today. We'll make camp here."

"Pretty bossy, aren't you, Doctor?" Edge grinned.

Nevertheless, she knew he was still weak. And she suspected that the struggle with the scaled monster had truly been worse than anything else he had ever endured.

"All right, then," he said. "Dai, you go see if you can scout out some water."

"Yes sir!"

While Dai was gone, Jaleel made a quick trek toward a low-lying bluff that rose against the horizon. She came back quickly, saying, "We're in good luck. There's a *cave* over there."

"I just hope none of those dragons are in it," Dr. Cole said rather fearfully.

"I saw nothing. Well, here comes Dai. Come along and bring the captain, and we'll get a fire going. Maybe I can go out and shoot something so that we can have fresh meat again."

Edge's small group was gathered around a fire inside the cave. Unseen cracks in the rock were carrying off the smoke as Dai roasted some meat. Jaleel had killed a large bird, something like a turkey. As he poked at the meat to test its tenderness, he said, "I like this cave. It beats being out in the open."

"I don't know," Jaleel said, a worried look on her smooth dark face. "It's occurred to me that we're trapped in here if anyone comes. There's no way out. No back door to this cave."

"I wonder who made it?" Dr. Cole said. She was sitting across from Edge, and he had noticed her watching his face from time to time. Now she looked toward where the cave made a turn in the rock behind them. "It's not a natural cavern, is it?"

"Oh, I expect it is," Edge said. "See how sandy the rock is? There was probably a river here at one time that ate out this cave."

"I think the turkey's about ready," Dai announced. He had cut up the bird and roasted the pieces on small sticks. He handed part of the breast to the doctor and another part to Edge. "White meat for you," he said cheerfully. He grinned over at Lieutenant Jaleel. "How about you, Lieutenant? White meat or dark?"

"I like the legs."

"So do I. One for you," Dai handed over a stick that had impaled on it a fat leg and now was dripping with juice. "And one for me—unless Raina prefers a leg. Watch it. It's hot."

"I like the wings," Raina said. "Nobody else ever likes them, so I always was able to have my own way."

The five sat back and ate hungrily. It had been a hard march, and the dried food that they had brought with them did not seem to satisfy.

Darkness fell outside the cave like a curtain falling, and when Edge glanced outside, he could not see even one star in the sky.

Jaleel took this as a benefit, however. "As dark as it is, no one will be prowling around tonight unless it's some animal. We'd better have a guard. I'll take the first watch."

"Let me do it," Dai said. "I'm not sleepy."

Jaleel shook her head. "No. I'll do the first watch. You can relieve me at midnight."

"All right, Lieutenant. I'll do that."

After Jaleel took her post by the entrance of the cave, Raina wandered a little deeper into the cave to roll up in her blanket. Dai Bando began shoring up the fire with large chunks of dead wood that he had dragged in. Soon it was flickering brightly again, and he sat with his back against the stone wall and stared into it. Then he began singing an ancient song under his breath. He had a beautiful singing voice. The song had a mournful tune, but somehow, to Edge, watching him, Dai did not seem sad as he sang:

"On top of Old Smoky, all covered with snow,
I lost my true lover for courtin' too slow.
Now, courtin's a pleasure, but parting is grief,
And a false-hearted lover is worse than a thief;

"For a thief will just rob you and take what you have,
But a false-hearted lover will lead to the grave;
And the grave will decay you, and turn you to dust.
Not one boy in a hundred a poor girl can trust.
They'll hug you and kiss you and tell you more lies
Than the cross ties on a railroad or stars in the skies.

"So, come, all you young maidens and listen to me:
Never place your affections in a green willow tree;
For the leaves they will wither, and the roots they
     will die.
Your lover will forsake you, and you'll never know
     why."

As the doleful song ended, Mark Edge looked over and saw a strange expression on the face of his surgeon. "What is it, Temple?" he asked quietly. "You don't like that song?"

Stirring her shoulders as if disturbed, Temple dropped her head. She looked into the fire for so long that at first Edge thought she had not heard his question. When she did look up, there was tremendous sadness in her large eyes. She said, almost in a whisper, "I guess I'm sad because it's a true song."

"A true song? What does that mean?"

"Didn't you hear what it said? 'A false-hearted lover is worse than a thief.'"

They sat in silence then, listening to the fire crackle and watching the flames ascend toward the roof of the cave. In fact, they sat so long that Dai Bando moved away, wrapped himself in his blanket, and fell asleep with the ease of a cat.

When the boy's breathing was regular, Edge said, "It sounds to me like you've had a hard time with a man somewhere along your way."

Temple Cole shrugged, but her lips grew tight. "I really don't want to talk about it, Mark," she said shortly.

"Sometimes it helps to talk. What's the matter? Did some man let you down?"

"Yes! A man let me down, and I'll never forgive him —never!" She walked away from the fire then, rolled up in her blanket, and turned her face to the wall.

Edge watched with her with shock, for he had not seen this side of Temple Cole before. He sat for a while longer, thinking of his own feelings. *Somewhere along the line she got a pretty bad jolt. I guess I know a little bit about that,* he thought ironically. Then he too went to sleep.

The fire died down to a bed of glowing red coals as Jaleel kept watch at the entrance. Outside there were the occasional night sounds of birds and of large animals prowling.

Dai Bando sat at the mouth of the cave from midnight until almost dawn. He was growing sleepy. At last the first thin lines of light began to appear in the east, and he stretched and went inside. The others were still asleep, and he began quietly laying small sticks on the fire to rekindle it. It was his intention to roast some more of the turkey for breakfast before they left.

He had just gotten the fire blazing when he heard a sound outside. He whirled, fully alert.

Then Dai's shout filled the cave. "Get up! We're being attacked!"

Captain Edge came to his feet—he had that quality of coming out of a sound sleep to full awareness almost instantly.

A group of ten or twelve men, roughly dressed and all carrying weapons, stood at the cave entrance. They were older weapons, the kind that fired bits of metal rather than the more sophisticated kind.

Edge's hand darted down to the holster where his Neuromag nestled, but an explosion rang out, and he felt a bullet pass beside his ear so closely that he could hear it whistling.

"Hold it right there!"

Jaleel also had come awake quickly, as had Temple Cole and Raina. Now the five of them stood looking down the muzzles of the weapons held by the men who had invaded their cave.

Edge took a deep breath as he looked the group over. The men were nothing out of the ordinary. Some planets had produced giants and others dwarfs such as lived on Ivan Petroski's home planet, Bellinka. But these men appeared all fairly normal. Their hair was long, and most of them were bearded, but not the one who was clearly the leader.

"We come in peace," Mark said quickly, holding his palm upward in the universal peace sign. He hoped desperately that they spoke the common language of the galaxy. Otherwise, without Mei-Lani Lao they would be helpless.

"Who are you? What are you doing in our land?"

The speaker was the clean-shaven man, slightly taller than the others. He had dark blue eyes, and his hair was fair. His arms were muscular, and there was a look of authority about him.

"I'm Mark Edge, captain of the *Daystar.*"

The leader hesitated, eyeing him. "What is the *Daystar?*" he demanded.

"A spaceship. We come from Earth."

"You're lying!" the tall blond man said. "Spaceships do not land here. They land at the capital, Merlina City."

Captain Edge exchanged glances with Lieutenant Jaleel, and a message seemed to pass between them. It was the question of how much to reveal to these men. If they were servants of the wizards, it would be wise not to reveal much. On the other hand, they did not *look* like wizards . . .

Edge said, "I'm on an exploratory mission. We were headed for Merlina City, but we became lost."

"I do not believe you! You are spies from the Grand Wizard! You might as well tell the truth!"

Spies from the Grand Wizard? This implied to Mark Edge that these men, whoever they were, were not on friendly terms with the wizards. He said, "No, we're not allied with the wizards in any way." Then he decided to take a big risk. "We've come because our government has heard that there are problems on your planet." Taking a deep breath, he added, "They suspect that the wizards are using dark arts to overcome other peoples."

A hubbub of whispering behind the leader was easily audible, but the leader held up his hands and cut it off. He continued to stare at the captives. "We will talk more of this. My name is Rowdan."

"Are you the leader of your people?"

"We will not talk here. You will come to our village. We cannot let you go until we are certain that it would be safe."

"Why wouldn't it be safe?" Lieutenant Jaleel demanded. "We've told you we come as friends."

"When you have been on Merlina for a time," Rowdan said, fixing his gaze on the warrior woman, "you will discover that it is not wise to reveal all you know. In spite of what you say, you still may be servants of the wizards. And even if you are not, they have ways of knowing what goes on—even in dark caves such as this one."

"We only want to prove to you that we have no intentions of harming you."

"Hand over your weapons."

Jaleel said, "No."

But the captain said, "Lieutenant, hand over your weapon." He removed his Neuromag from its holster and extended it, butt first.

Rowdan took the Neuromag and handled it awkwardly. Then he looked at Mark and nodded for his men to collect the weapons of the others.

"Now we will go."

The man who had taken Dai's weapon said, "It was the Lord's mercy that we found them here, Rowdan."

Dai Bando smiled. "You're Christians, aren't you?"

Rowdan's eyes opened with surprise. "Yes," he said. "We are believers in the Christ."

"Then we are certainly not your enemies, Rowdan," Dai said. "We have come here to help your people fight against the forces of darkness, the servants of the Evil One."

Rowdan stared at the boy as if trying to read his thoughts. He said, "If that is true, you are welcome. Come. You will talk to our elders, and they will decide. But I must warn you, they are men of deep wisdom. If they decree that you aren't what you say, your lives are forfeit." He scowled then. "We are fighting against the wizards of Merlina. They have enslaved all free men, and we are determined to overthrow them. But they have strange powers, as you probably well know."

"We know very little, Rowdan," Captain Edge said quickly, "but we will welcome a meeting with your elders."

"Then come."

9

Council of War

Someone's coming!"

Jerusha looked at Ringo with surprise. The two were standing in the shadow of the *Daystar*, and apart from the usual noises coming from the ship, she could hear nothing. "Are you sure, Ringo? I don't hear anything."

Ringo tilted his head to one side. "Yes. I'm sure." He pulled his Neuromag from his belt. "We don't know who this is. It *may* be the scouting party coming back, but it may be someone else." He hesitated, then said, "No—wait. It's the captain."

Jerusha strained her eyes and after a few moments was able to see tiny figures emerging from a distant line of trees. "You mean you heard them from that far away!" she exclaimed. "I never knew anyone with the senses that you have. You can see farther and hear better than anybody I ever knew."

"It's a good thing I can do something right," Ringo murmured. He was staring at the group. "They're not alone. There are others with them. Better alert the ship."

By the time the scouting party reached the *Daystar*, everyone aboard was watching, either from inside or having come out to watch.

"Well, they picked up some company!" Heck declared, standing next to Jerusha. "They look like pretty primitive types, don't they?"

The captain, by this time, had come within hailing

distance. "Hello, *Daystar!* Scouting party returning."
He came up to the officers. "This is Rowdan. Rowdan,
let me introduce you to my crew." He went over the
names, and as he did, Rowdan studied their faces,
seeming more interested in them than in the ship itself.

"Come inside, you and your people, Rowdan. I'm
sure we could all stand something to eat. Ensign Ericson, could you get the cook to stir up a quick meal for
us?"

"Yes sir. At once."

Thirty minutes later, the visitors were seated at
one of the long tables in the mess hall. Captain Edge
was sitting across from the leader, and after the meal
had gone on for some time, he said, "What do you think
of the ship, Rowdan?"

"I don't know much about things like this. We're
not a scientific people." Rowdan looked around curi-
ously. "It's all beyond me."

"Perhaps one advantage of our visit here will be to
give you some help. Maybe we can make life easier
with a few scientific conveniences."

Rowdan glanced at the woman who had come
with him. This was Lanie, his wife. She evidently
worked closely with her husband. She was a tall
woman with the same light hair and blue eyes as most
of the Merlinians. They were a handsome people,
quick, alert, and physically strong and active.

She said quietly, "It isn't conveniences we need so
much as deliverance."

The woman's statement puzzled Edge. He blinked
and ran a hand across his blond hair, trying to think.
"Deliverance. You sound like captives, yet you're walking around free."

"No, we're not," Lanie said, and there was a sadness about her. "We are more imprisoned, Captain Edge, than if we were in a dungeon."

"I don't understand that," Edge said, "but in any case perhaps we could help. We could send back to Earth for more space cruisers and bring a small army here. A force from the Intergalactic Council would wipe out any opposition the wizards may offer."

"It's not quite that easy, Captain," Rowdan said. "You don't have any idea how powerful the wizards are! They can kill with a curse as quickly as your people can with some of your sophisticated weapons."

Edge toyed with his knife.

"And you don't believe that, do you, Captain?" Lanie said. "Do you think we're making it all up?"

"Well . . . of course not," Edge stammered. "But I just haven't had experience with these things."

Bronwen Llewellen had been sitting quietly, listening to the talk as it ran around the table. Now she spoke up, bringing everyone's eyes to her. Her silver hair framed a face dominated by her dark blue eyes. "I think you'd better pay attention to what our guests are saying, Captain Edge. I have encountered this sort of thing before, and it's never pleasant. If the wizards are in league with the Devil, then their powers will be great indeed."

Temple Cole studied the small figure of Bronwen Llewellen. "Surely you don't believe that, Bronwen. All those myths and fairytales about the Devil?"

Bronwen gave her a steady gaze. "To one who hasn't encountered occult power, it does seem unbelievable, but the Scriptures tell us plainly that Jesus spent a great deal of time casting out demons. You may not believe that record, but I know it to be true."

Her calm assurance shook the demeanor of the captain. He had come to have tremendous confidence in this older woman, and it was obvious that she was totally convinced that tremendous spiritual powers were about to be unleashed.

"Again, why did you really come here, Captain?" Lanie asked. "I know you have said you came to explore, but you also suggested that there is more to it than that."

For a moment Edge hesitated, then nodded. "Commandant Winona Lee believes that if the power of the wizards is not contained, they may do tremendous damage in the galaxy."

"Didn't you say, Captain," Jerusha said, "that Commandant Lee believes it's possible they may grow so powerful they could take over the galaxy?"

"Well, I don't think it could go *that* far." Edge reached for a glass of water, drank, then put the glass down. "But Commandant Lee certainly wants us to do what we can to stop that from ever being attempted."

Silence ran around the table until Rowdan said, "If the wizards are stopped, it will not be with weapons. It will be with spiritual power." He looked around until his gaze fell on Raina St. Clair. The two seemed to exchange some unspoken communication. Rowdan smiled. "I feel that you are one who might be helpful in such a struggle, Ensign St. Clair."

Raina's face flushed. "I thank you for your confidence, Rowdan. I do believe that the power of God is greater than the power of evil, and I agree that if demons are involved, our weapons will not avail. It must be through the power of Jesus."

"I agree with that," Mei-Lani said. She was so small and so quiet that it was easy to ignore her.

Lanie, sitting next to her, suddenly reached over and put her hand over that of the small girl.

"I feel that you too understand what is happening, Mei-Lani."

Mei-Lani smiled at the blonde woman. "In my studies I have found that throughout history there has always been the power of good against evil. And there have always been terrible men and women who have arisen. Men such as Stalin and Hitler lived in the ancient days, men who obviously possessed great power that was not their own. And even the short time I have been on Merlina, I have felt the force of evil. There is a darkness on this planet . . ." She shivered slightly. "It must be awful to live here under such forces."

"It *is* awful," Rowdan said. He smiled then. "But I have hope, now that you are here. It is good to know that there are other Christians who will help." He looked over at Dai Bando. "This boy here is such a one. Physically he is the strongest young man I've ever seen, but inwardly he has another strength. And I believe it comes from God."

Tara Jaleel watched and listened in silence. The conversation around the table was foreign talk to her, for she did not believe in a personal almighty God, much less in a Devil. Later she said to Studs Cagney, "Do you believe all that about God and the Devil and demons?" Her eyes were angry, for something in the meeting had challenged her.

Studs stroked his thick brown hair with a heavy hand. "I don't know," he said. "But I'll tell you one thing. Mei-Lani's right about this planet. I've been on lots of them, and I've never felt such danger. There's something here that I don't like." He scowled. "Whatever it is, we're going to have to go up against it, and I don't feel good about it."

"I don't know what to think about all of this," Ringo said. "Talk about demons and devils bothers me."

Raina was seated beside Ringo. The others were gone. She had loosed her auburn hair so that it fell over her shoulders, and now she ran her hand over it in an unconscious gesture. "It bothers me too, Ringo. The Devil's activity is not anything to treat lightly. I think we're going to have a terrible battle here, and some of us may not survive."

Ringo glanced at her. "Are you afraid, Raina?"

"Afraid? No, there's nothing to be afraid of as long as we're in God's hands. Once you turn yourself over to Jesus Christ, there's nothing that can happen that He doesn't control."

Ringo was silent. He was a believer but a very weak one indeed. He had noticed that there was a strength in some of the crew members that he did not have. "I wish I could feel like that," he said, "but I never have. I've always felt out of place and not equal to whatever was expected of me."

"You've made a place for yourself with the *Daystar* Ensigns," Raina said. "You shouldn't put yourself down so much." Raina reached over and took his hand. Her green eyes were warm. "I think you're neat, Ringo." She squeezed his hand, got up, and left the mess hall.

Ringo looked after her, thinking, *That's the best thing she's ever said to me.* Then he stood. *I'm not neat, though, no matter what she says.* He desperately wanted acceptance and love, but he didn't know how to receive it or give it. He walked sadly away, wondering if he would ever find a way to express his feelings.

For two days Rowdan and Lanie remained on the *Daystar.* They showed some interest in the technical side of the ship but more in the people. Lanie became quite close to Mei-Lani Lao, and the two of them spent hours together.

Dai Bando said once, "What do you two find to talk about, Mei-Lani?"

"Oh, just things."

Dai was shifting some cargo, moving heavy cartons around as though they were filled with feathers. He was interested in the relationship between the girl and the older woman. "Do you like her? Lanie, I mean?"

"Yes, I do. And she's a fine Christian. She has spiritual gifts that I never encountered before."

"Spiritual gifts? What's that?"

"Oh, you know. God gives people abilities. He enables them to do things that they couldn't do in the natural."

"I don't guess I have any of those."

"But you do," Mei-Lani said. "Every believer has something from God. You're very strong, and that's a gift. And you're kind too, and that's a gift from God."

Putting down a carton, Dai turned to scrutinize her. He had always liked Mei-Lani's looks. She was small and dainty and had the blackest possible hair. He liked the almond shape of her eyes. They were large and expressive. "Well, *you've* certainly got gifts," he said.

"All I do is read books and study languages."

"No, it's more than that. You've been kind to me ever since you first met me. And if it weren't for you, I wouldn't have gotten to come on the *Daystar*. Everybody else can do electronics or computers. All I can do is pick up boxes."

Mei-Lani shook her head. "That's not true, Dai. You have a beautiful singing voice. There's nothing I love more than hearing you sing the old hymns."

101

Dai's prominent dimples leaped into place. "Singing and picking up boxes. I guess that's about my limit. And by the way, what do you think the captain will do next?"

"I have no idea," Mei-Lani said. "Of course, it's impossible to lead a revolt. We're only one ship, and this is a whole planet."

"Well, the captain will think of something," Dai said confidently. "He's really cool."

At almost the same moment that Dai was wondering what the captain would do, Dr. Temple Cole was asking the same question. She and Captain Edge were sitting in his cabin when the surgeon asked, "What are you going to do, Mark, about all of this?"

Understanding her meaning, Edge ran his hand through his hair in despair. "I don't know, Temple. I wish I could get in touch with the Commandant. Maybe she could give us some advice."

"I think you should go for a meeting with the wizards."

"*What?*"

"It's the only thing to do, isn't it?" Temple had been struggling with herself for some time but now had decided that, despite her rather uncertain feelings about Mark Edge, she was going to pursue her arrangement with Sir Richard Irons.

She had been ready to throw over the whole betrayal thing, but for two nights in a row, as she slept, something had hardened her heart. Now she was totally committed. *I've got to get him in contact with the wizards. They'll know what to do. Then I can get my money and be out of this thing.*

Now she said, "After all, we've got to contact the wizards somehow. I'll go with you, Mark. Together we can talk to them, and at least find out what they're like."

Edge was obviously still uncertain.

"Anyhow," she said, "I think that's what we'll have to do."

"Let me think about it, and we'll see."

"All right, Mark."

Then she leaned across and touched his cheek. "We can do it, you and I. There's nothing we can't do if we work together." She drew his head down and kissed him.

After the doctor had left the cabin, Mark Edge sat down, puzzled. He was an uncomplicated man, who required action, and there had been none. The subtleties of all of this confused him. *I wish I knew what to do.* His mind was half on the beautiful Temple Cole and the other half was on the affair at hand.

"I'll have to make up my mind," he muttered. "But somehow I don't feel good about all of this."

10

The Captain Makes a Choice

Practically the entire crew of the *Daystar* was gathered outside on a fine Sunday morning. They had been joined by most of the resistance movement, including many women and children, so that the clearing was filled. The service had come about as a result of Mei-Lani's talk with Lanie.

The tall, blond chief of the Merlinians arose and began to speak.

Captain Edge had reluctantly agreed to attend. He stood at the back of the crowd, his form towering over the others, and Jerusha, who was across the way, studied him. *He didn't want to do this*, she thought. *He's afraid of anything spiritual—which is a shame.*

Rowdan had a clear voice that carried easily, and in his hand he held a book. "I'm happy that we are able to meet together and worship God with our friends," he said with a smile. "It has encouraged all of us here who have grown sad over the struggle which we appear to be losing. Now—" he looked at the *Daystar* crew "— God has brought other believers here to join with us in our struggle. I thank God for manifesting Himself in this way, and I would like for us to sing together a song celebrating the power of Jesus Christ and of the Father and of the Holy Spirit."

Dai was standing with Mei-Lani, listening as Rowdan led the Merlinians in a simple song. Dai had never heard it before, but when Rowdan started singing the song again, Dai joined in with the others. His voice rose above the music made by all the rest.

When the hymn was finished, Rowdan smiled at him. "God has given you a great gift—a voice such as I have never heard. Perhaps you would sing some of your Earth songs celebrating the Christ for us?"

Dai began to sing. His voice had a warm, intimate quality as he sang a song that his aunt had taught him. It was an old song, she had said, but had been sung by Christians for thousands of years:

"On a hill far away stood an old rugged cross,
The emblem of suffering and shame,
And I love that old cross where the dearest and best
For a world of lost sinners was slain . . ."

When the last strains of Dai's song died away, Mei-Lani covertly wiped away tears. "That was beautiful, Dai!" she whispered. "I'm always moved when you sing like that."

The service went on. The Merlinian pastor read from his Bible, which was the same as the one that the Christians on the *Daystar* used. Then he preached. After the service, the two groups—crew and Merlinians—visited together, and those who were Christians found fellowship that pleased and surprised them all.

Captain Edge, however, had disappeared.

Finding Zeno Thrax, Edge said, "What do you make of all that, Zeno?"

"I don't know, Captain. I'm not a Christian myself, but there's a goodness about these people that attracts me strongly. What did you think?"

Whatever the captain had thought, he didn't say,

for Dr. Cole suddenly appeared. She said, "How about a walk, Captain?"

"Fine. Commander Thrax, you're in charge of the ship."

"Yes, sir." Thrax watched the two stroll off in the direction of the trees that lay over to their left. He was puzzled again by his inability to even guess what was on the doctor's mind.

When Jerusha came later to the bridge, he said, "I simply can't make that woman out—Dr. Cole, I mean." His colorless eyes looked bewildered. "I've never seen anyone quite like her. She's beautiful and charming—but there's something . . . strange about her."

"I couldn't agree more, Zeno," Jerusha said. She was off duty so was not wearing her uniform. Instead she wore a lightweight garment made of green silk, belted at the waist with a single black cord. Her ash blonde hair hung down her back. She sat down beside the first officer and frowned. "And I'm worried about what's going to happen."

"Why are you worried?" Zeno asked. "I think we're doing very well. I don't understand the Christian viewpoint, but I'm studying it carefully. Mei-Lani gave me a copy of the Christian Scriptures, and I've been reading it every night."

"What do you think?" Jerusha asked.

"I'm fascinated by Jesus. I've read extensively, but I've never heard of any man like Him."

"There *is* no one else like Him." Jerusha smiled. She liked the first officer very much. For a while she talked about the Scriptures, but eventually her mind went back to the captain.

"Zeno, I'm worried about Captain Edge. He's not himself."

"You're correct. He's not himself. I've been with

him on many missions, and he's never been like this. You know what it is, of course."

"Well, of course! He's completely *infatuated* with that woman!" She tossed her head, sending her hair cascading across her back. "He's not reasonable about that woman."

"From what I read, love is not a reasonable thing," Zeno commented. "I've never been in love myself, so I can't say. But I do believe the captain is making some mistakes in judgment."

"Then why don't you tell him, Zeno?"

"I have attempted to, but it appears I can't get through to him as I once could."

They talked quietly for a while longer. Then Jerusha said, "I'm going to walk my dog."

Zeno said, "I wouldn't do that if I were you."

"What? Go for a walk?"

"That's not all you have in mind. You have in mind to challenge the captain and tell him he's wrong about Dr. Cole."

A flush came to Jerusha's face. She could never quite get used to being analyzed by the first officer. And furthermore, she could not deny it, for that was exactly what was on her mind.

"Somebody's got to tell him what a fool he's making of himself."

"I don't think that would be wise," Zeno said. "Men don't like to be told that they're doing foolish things." He watched her walk off the bridge. A few minutes later he saw her leave the ship with Contessa and head toward the trees that lay beyond.

"I'm afraid Jerusha's in for trouble," he murmured. "She's fonder of the captain than she knows—and perhaps fonder than she should be."

The big German shepherd darted here and there, barking at the small animals that appeared among the trees. Then she bounded back to Jerusha's side.

"You like this, don't you, girl?" Leaning over, Jerusha patted the broad head, then picked up a stick and threw it. Contessa went crashing through the bushes and brought back a different stick. "That's not the one," she said, laughing, "but it'll do."

For some time she exercised Contessa, then continued her walk. When they came to a stream, Contessa plunged in, swimming strongly to the other side, then back again. It was a pleasant walk, and Jerusha always enjoyed being out with her dog.

When she started back to the *Daystar*, almost at once she came upon the captain and Dr. Cole. The two had been sitting together on a fallen tree, and both jumped up as Jerusha and Contessa suddenly appeared.

"Oh, it's you, Ensign," Edge said, with a guilty look on his face.

"Hello, Captain. Hello, Dr. Cole."

Jerusha would have passed on, but then a strange thing happened.

The captain and the doctor were still standing side by side. Suddenly Contessa lowered her head and began to walk stiff-legged toward them. She pushed herself between them, causing Edge to stagger as the weight of the heavy dog hit his lower legs.

"What are you doing? Get away! Ensign, get this animal away from me!"

"Contessa, come here."

But Contessa did not obey. There was a low growl in her throat, and her eyes were fixed on the surgeon.

Dr. Cole took a step backward, alarm on her face. "Ensign Ericson, get this animal away!" she ordered harshly.

"Contessa!" Jerusha's voice was sharp. "Come here at once."

Contessa gave the doctor one more look, growled, and then moved reluctantly away. She came to Jerusha's side, but her eyes were still fixed on the surgeon's face. The dog did make a threatening sight.

"What's *wrong* with that dog?" Temple Cole exclaimed nervously. "She never has liked me!"

"She's very possessive, and she likes the captain very much," Jerusha said. She turned away, saying, "I'm sorry to have disturbed your visit."

When they were out of earshot, Jerusha muttered, "Visit—*ha!* I'm going to talk to him about what he's doing. I don't care what happens."

Later on that day she was still thinking about what to say to Mark Edge. Finally she went to Bronwen Llewellen and explained what had happened. "Contessa couldn't stand that woman!" she finally exclaimed. "She's got more sense than the captain!"

Bronwen was sitting in her cabin. Its only decorations were a few mementos of her late husband, a large picture of Dai, and the painting that hung at the head of her bunk.

"I think it would be a mistake for you to go to the captain with this," Bronwen said.

"Well, *somebody's* got to talk some sense into him."

"Sometimes women have a strange power over men. You find it all through the Scriptures. Look at the man whom God loved so greatly, David. He fell under the power of Bathsheba, and she wasn't even trying to entice him. And, of course, Samson had great gifts, but he was unable to resist Delilah. It's both the strength of men and the weakness of men somehow."

"What do you mean, Bronwen?"

"Men are drawn to women because of their needs, but they are weakened because they sometimes fall under the power of women who are not good. Men aren't always able to draw the distinction. Especially men like Captain Edge. He's a good man but not a godly man, and he has no spiritual discernment. He sees that she's beautiful and charming, and that's all he knows."

"Do you think she's . . . evil?"

Bronwen hesitated. "I think she's very confused. She is not a woman who has given her heart to God. That can be a dangerous thing when a woman is both beautiful and intelligent."

"Well, I'm going to talk to him, anyway," Jerusha said firmly. She got up and left, her back straight with determination.

Captain Edge called a meeting immediately after the evening meal. He said, "All officers and ensigns will meet with me in the war room." He strolled away, and Jerusha's heart beat faster. "He's made up his mind," she said to Raina. "And I'm afraid of what he's going to do."

When they were all gathered in the war room, Edge stood up and said, "I've made a decision. We can't just stay here indefinitely, so I've decided to go and meet with the wizards."

A murmur went around the room, and Jerusha exclaimed, "But, Captain, that can be very dangerous!"

"I'm not sure that it will be, but it's a risk that we will have to take."

For some time the group discussed the need for contacting the wizards and finding out exactly who they were. Captain Edge overruled all objections. He said, "Dr. Cole and I feel that it is something that must be done. We will leave at first light in the morning."

"Dr. Cole!" Jerusha spoke aloud before she could think, and every eye turned to her. "Wouldn't it be better, Captain, to take . . ." She wanted to say, "Take some godly people with you to combat the forces of evil." But finally she said, "To take someone with more experience?"

"Dr. Cole and I will handle the situation," Edge said shortly. "This meeting is adjourned."

Ringo and Heck managed to hide themselves, for Lieutenant Jaleel had scheduled them both for another Jain Jayati session. Sitting in the cargo hold, they hoped that Jaleel would forget about it. Heck had brought a bagful of sweets and popcorn and was eating both at the same time.

Watching him, Ringo said, "That's disgusting!"

"What's disgusting?"

"Mixing all that stuff up together, popcorn and caramels."

"All goes to the same place, and I like both of them," Heck said cheerfully. Suddenly he turned to Ringo and said, "You're really stuck on Raina, aren't you?"

"No, I'm not!"

"Sure you are. I can tell."

"You don't know anything about it."

"I know *all* about love. I'm an expert."

"I haven't noticed any of the girls hanging around you."

"They're afraid of me. They know what power I have when I unleash my full charm." Heck leaned back and patted his pudgy stomach. "I can tell you what you're doing wrong—for a slight fee."

"What are you talking about—'for a slight fee'?"

"Well, experts get paid for what they know. So for fifty dollars, I'll tell you what you need to know about how to make Raina fall in love with you."

"No."

"All right, I'll give you the advice anyway. When you see how well it works, you'll come across with the money. What you have to do is play your cards right. Women are all alike. You do certain things, and they'll fall for you."

Despite himself, Ringo was interested.

"They like to be told that they're pretty, that they're sweet, that there's nobody else in the world like them. Stuff like that. You can even write them a poem."

"I can't write poetry."

"Steal one. There's plenty of poems around. Just put your name at the bottom. Who's to know?"

Ringo scowled. "You're a low-down scoundrel!"

"Why do you say that?" Heck was hurt. "I'm trying to tell you how to get what you want. You want Raina to like you? This is the way. Hey, where you going?"

"Away from you."

Ringo got up and walked off, but he was thinking, *Maybe a poem would help, but I won't steal it. I'll write it myself.*

Jerusha knew she had to act quickly. If the captain and Dr. Cole were leaving in the morning, she would have to see him tonight. She kept a close watch and saw that, as usual, the doctor went to the captain's cabin that evening. She hung around, waiting until at last, very late, the woman left. As soon as she was out of sight, Jerusha went to the captain's door and knocked.

"Who is it?"

"Ensign Ericson."

The door opened with a hiss, then closed behind her. "Captain, I need to talk to you."

"It's late, Jerusha. Won't tomorrow do?"

"No. It has to be now." Jerusha took a deep breath. "Captain, please don't go tomorrow."

Edge looked surprised. "What do you mean 'don't go'? I've got to go."

"Then, at least don't take Dr. Cole with you. Take Raina, or better still, Bronwen—or both of them."

"Why should I take *them?*"

"Captain, haven't you been listening?" she exclaimed. "Everyone has told us these wizards have tremendous powers, and they're not good powers. You need strong believers there with you to protect you from what the wizards might do."

She could tell that Edge was displeased. All evening Dr. Cole had probably been impressing on him what a wise thing it was for the two of them to go.

"My decision has been made. It'll be all right. You don't need to be concerned."

Jerusha's temper flared. "Captain, you're infatuated with that woman!"

"What did you say?"

"You heard me, Captain! You're so blinded by her, you can't even think straight! You're not acting like a captain! You're acting like a child!"

"Get out of my cabin! *You're* a child! I wish I'd left you in that crummy room where I found you!"

"You know you're wrong, Captain."

"You're jealous. That's what your problem is!"

There was just enough truth in his words to stop Jerusha dead still. She felt tears come into her eyes. Rather than let him see, she turned away blindly. "You're going to regret this, Captain Edge. It's going to

114

be the biggest mistake you ever made in your life. That woman is evil, and you're going to pay for your infatuation with her!"

The door closed behind Jerusha, and Captain Edge glowered at it. Confusion rushed through him, for he liked Jerusha Ericson, and he trusted her. Still, thoughts of Temple Cole came to his mind, and he grunted, "Jerusha's wrong this time. She just doesn't like Temple."

He prepared for bed, his mind full of plans for the next day. But he kept hearing Jerusha's accusation: *"That woman is evil!"* He determined to close his mind to it all, muttering, "She's just a child. She doesn't know anything." Still, he slept badly, his sleep troubled with dreams, and when he arose the next morning he was exhausted.

11

Council of the Grand Wizards

Merlina City caught Captain Edge off guard. He had heard so much about the planet's backwardness in the realm of scientific technology that he had been expecting a shabby sort of town. But when they reached the gates, he said to Temple, "They may not be much on weapons, but they know how to build a city."

The buildings were magnificent. Tall spires reached high into the heavens. Turrets with golden roofs gleamed and glittered. Most of the structures seemed made of white marble, so that there was a fairytale look about the city.

"It is beautiful, isn't it?" Temple murmured. "No one allied to demons or the Devil could build a city like this."

"No. They'd be more likely to hole up in a dark cave. This makes me feel better. I think all of this business about dark powers has been overrated. Jerusha and the other Christians are nice people, but they do get carried away with religion sometimes."

At the moment he stopped speaking, a dark-faced man dressed in a silver and black uniform approached them.

"What is your business here?" he demanded.

"My name is Captain Mark Edge. This is my associate, Dr. Cole. We would like to see the Grand Wizards."

The guard gazed at him thoughtfully, then said, "Come this way. I will see if the wizards will allow your visit."

"Strange sort of guard—if he is one," Mark said, as they followed the man. "He doesn't even carry a weapon."

The Merlinian took them down a broad street that led straight to the highest tower. It rose toward the sky, seemingly unendingly, and Mark had to crane his neck to see the top.

"Nothing more impressive than this on Earth, is there, Temple?"

"No, I think not."

The guard escorted them to a small room where they were scrutinized by two other soldiers wearing the same black and silver uniform. After a lengthy wait, he returned and said, "You will come this way."

"What is this called? This building?" Mark asked.

"You do not know? This is the High Tower. My name is Menton. I am one of the servants of the Grand Wizards."

"Do you think we might be able to see the wizards today?" Mark asked.

"That is as they command. In the meanwhile, I am to see that you have suitable quarters."

The quarters were, indeed, suitable. Mark and Temple were each shown to a large and well-furnished room.

Menton said, "Now you will wait until the Grand Wizard condescends to see you."

"How long do you think that will be?"

"It is not for me to say. I will have food brought to you at once."

The guard left them standing in the room assigned to the captain. Here the walls were of a peach-colored substance, much like marble, and the furniture was made of beautifully designed wood.

Mark went to a window. "Come here and look down," he said.

Temple joined him and looked out. They had a view of the entire city. "Beautiful," she said.

118

"Look over there, though." Mark pointed to his right. "It's not all beautiful. That looks like a pretty bad section."

"Probably where the workers live," Temple murmured.

An attendant brought a tray then, and she went over to lift a silver cover. "This food looks all right," she said. "Shall we try some?"

"Sounds good to me. I'm hungry."

The meal consisted of meat and an unfamiliar vegetable. The drink was a heady liquid that had a delicious taste. When they had finished eating, Mark leaned back and grinned. "Obviously we won't starve to death here."

"Let's go take a walk around," she said, throwing down her napkin.

But as soon as they opened the door, two guards planted themselves in front of them.

"We just want to walk around a little bit," Mark explained.

"You're not permitted to do that."

The guards were pale men with glittering eyes. There was a strange look about them that Mark could not identify. Neither of them had weapons, and the captain said pleasantly, "Well, we're just going to go outside and walk around." He started down the hallway. "Come along, Temple—"

Suddenly he found himself imprisoned in some sort of way he could not understand. The guards had not moved, though both were watching him. He felt pain in his chest, which grew steadily worse.

Temple rushed to him, saying, "Mark, are you all right?"

"Pain—pain in my chest."

"Here. Let me help you back into the room."

He leaned on her heavily, for the pain was intense.

"Lie down, and let me look you over," she said.

Mark slumped onto the bed and felt her lift his feet. She felt for his pulse. "I wish I had some instruments here!"

"It's getting a little better now."

"What was it? Tell me about it."

"I can't, exactly—it was like nothing I ever had before. It was like a huge fist squeezing me."

"That sounds like a heart attack, but your heart sounds good and strong. I don't think it was that."

The incident was troubling. When he could sit up, they talked about it for a while. And then Mark said, "Temple, this place is beautiful, but something's wrong with it. Those guards didn't have a weapon, but I think they put some sort of *spell* on me."

"Now you're talking like Bronwen," Temple admonished him. "I don't believe the guards had anything to do with it."

Mark did not argue, but he still felt pressure on his chest. He remembered that there had also been a sense of blackness and evil. He did not mention that to her.

The two of them were tired, and soon Temple left for her room. "Get some rest. In the morning we'll see the wizards, I'm sure."

Mark removed his outer clothes, lay down on the bed, and tried to sleep, but the effort was not successful. He tossed and turned. Edge was not a man who dreamed a great deal, and the images that floated into his mind were nightmarish. He finally he gave up and sat in a chair until dawn.

"Something's surely wrong here," he muttered.

Breakfast was brought early the next morning. As they sat at the table in Mark's room and ate, she looked at him critically. "You look tired. Didn't you sleep well?"

120

"I've slept better."

"Was there still some pain?" she asked.

"Not exactly. Just bad dreams."

At that moment the door opened, and Menton walked in. "You will come with me now. The Grand Wizards are in council. They have commanded that you be brought before them."

"Fine." Edge got to his feet and, with Temple at his side, followed the guard. This time they did not take the steps. An elevator swiftly carried them to the very top of the tower.

Stepping off the lift, he saw more guards dressed in black and silver. "What's that sign on their chests, Temple? I don't recognize it."

"Neither do I, but they all have it."

"It looks like a root—or maybe a broken upside-down cross. I never saw it before."

They were ushered into a large room where six people sat at a table, facing them. The man in the center was dressed in solid white. The others wore black and silver.

"My name is Melchior," the man in white said. He rose and bowed. "Welcome to Merlina." He was a handsome man, about sixty years of age, Mark guessed, and was at least six feet tall. He had hair completely silver, and he had strange eyes, the color of which was impossible to determine.

Beside him sat an imposing woman with coal black hair and eyes and narrow lips. She said, "My name is Iona. I am the Chief Sorceress of Merlina."

"I am Captain Mark Edge of the cruiser *Daystar*. This is my surgeon, Dr. Temple Cole."

"You are welcome. Both of you. Our council has met to hear what you have to say."

Edge ran his eyes over the council members. The other four all bore the symbol of the broken cross on their chests, and there was some further odd similarity about them all.

"We have been sent on a mission to bring greetings from Commandant Winona Lee of the Intergalactic Council," Mark said.

"We are happy to receive word from Commandant Lee," Melchior said smoothly. "Come. Sit down and give us a report in full."

For the next fifteen minutes Mark did his best to avoid the real purpose of their mission. The last thing he wanted was for Melchior and the sorceress to understand exactly what Commandant Lee had suspected—that this planet was the source of potential trouble in the galaxy. Instead, he tried to present his mission simply as an offer of peace.

He ended by saying, "We bring you greetings from the Intergalactic Council, and it is the hope of Commandant Lee that our two peoples can work much closer together."

There was quiet for a moment, and Mark felt as if he were being examined under a microscope. The eyes of the council members, particularly those of the sorceress and Melchior, were probing into him. He hoped desperately that they were not telepathic.

Then Melchior smiled. "You will be our guest, Captain Edge. We will meet often, and in the meantime we extend you the hospitality of Merlina."

Mark and Temple were escorted back to their quarters, but this time Menton said, "Chief Wizard Lord Melchior says that you are to be entertained. It will be my privilege to show you the city. If there is anything you desire, please do not hesitate to ask for it."

"Thank you, Menton," Mark said. When the guard left, he turned to the doctor. "That was some meeting, wasn't it?"

"What do you think, Mark?"

"Hard to say. They don't look like what the Christians have led me to believe. I thought they'd all be dressed in solid black and look terrible. They're actually nice-appearing people."

"I agree. Commandant Lee must have had some bad information. I think we'll be able to straighten it out, though. In the meanwhile, let's just enjoy ourselves."

Menton provided entertainment and food, and all day long Edge and the doctor were kept busy seeing the sights.

Late that afternoon, while Mark went with Menton to look at a special breed of horses that he was interested in, Temple returned to the High Tower, where she presented herself to a guard. "I have a special message for the Chief Wizard."

As if her coming had been expected, the doctor was taken at once to the top floor of the High Tower and escorted into the presence of the Chief Wizard. This time, only he and the sorceress were present.

"Ah!" Iona said, her eyes glittering. She was wearing a silver gown. "Dr. Cole, how nice to see you."

Temple said, "I must tell you that I am in the service of Sir Richard Irons."

"Indeed! That is interesting," Melchior murmured. He tilted his head to one side. "How can we be sure that you are telling us the truth?"

Suddenly Temple understood that he *knew* that she was telling the truth. There was something in this man that went beyond natural power. She knew that, despite her ability to shield her thoughts to a great extent, he had gone right to the heart of what she was.

"I think you know that I am telling the truth," she said. "You have heard from Sir Richard, I'm sure."

123

"Yes, we have," Iona replied and stood. "He informed us of your mission. Have you been successful?"

"Yes, have you been successful?" Melchior repeated. The wizard had a small mustache, and there was something odd about the shape of his eyes. "Have you been successful in making the captain fall in love with you?"

"So you *do* know. Well, I've done the best I can. But he's a strong man, and you'll find it difficult to change him."

"Oh, I think we can accomplish that," Melchior said. "It is not difficult for us to overcome those who don't believe in the dark powers. It is those who *do* believe and who look to—other sources of power— that we find difficult."

Temple felt that her mind was being bombarded with strong spiritual forces. She closed her eyes, swayed, and gritted her teeth. "I would appreciate it if you would not use your powers on me."

Iona laughed a tinkling metallic sound. "I can see you are strong as well. But you're on the right side. Sir Richard Irons tells me that we can trust you."

"You can do that. I'm being well paid."

"Well, then." Melchior arose and put a hand on Temple's shoulder. It was cold, and she shivered slightly, but he did not heed. "Now, we must get to business. It is our purpose to deceive Commandant Lee, as you know. First, the captain must be persuaded to deliver his ship here, to Merlina. And no report of what we are attempting to do here must go back to the commandant."

Temple stared into their faces. These people were so charming, and yet there *was* something evil about them. She knew it, and she asked in a whisper, "What are your goals?"

Melchior's glance crossed that of Iona, and then he smiled. "Nothing minor, my dear Dr. Cole. We simply want to rule the galaxy."

12

The Spell

Chief Wizard Melchior calling Sir Richard Irons . . ."
Sir Richard Irons listened to the soft voice speaking over the communications console. The linkup was extraordinary. Even though the message was being sent millions of miles through space, the Chief Wizard sounded as if he were in the room with Sir Richard.

Irons addressed the comm panel. "We have a good communication linkup finally," he said matter-of-factly.

"Thanks to the spatial repeaters your men installed. We've always discouraged new technology here, but I can see that we need to rethink our technological future. We are more accustomed to other ways."

Irons measured each word. "It's those 'other' ways that, along with our technology, will help us achieve our mutual goals."

"I am in full agreement. You will command the physical universe while we command the spiritual. We will be formidable allies."

"How are things progressing with Captain Edge and that crew of his?" Irons inquired.

"Our plans are working out exactly as we both desired." Melchior's voice was silky.

"So the good Dr. Cole is carrying out her part of the bargain?"

"Oh, yes, although we are watching her quite closely. I fear she is not as totally given over to our cause as you are, Sir Richard."

"No, but she's a selfish woman who was badly hurt in a love affair. Such a woman will do practically anything. She has made Edge fall in love with her, I assume."

"I think we can safely say that is true," Melchior replied.

"Well, then, all that remains to do is to see that Edge returns with a report that will please Commandant Lee. We must have more time, Melchior. We're not quite ready to launch our forces, and it is essential that we have that time."

"I do not feel that will be difficult, Sir Richard. As you may know, those who do not believe in the dark powers throw up no defenses, and, therefore, we can influence them quite easily. I do not think that Mark Edge will be much of a problem."

"And the woman?"

"Strangely enough, she has not yet completely given herself over to the powers that we hold—but she *will* do so, or else she must be destroyed."

Sir Richard Irons glanced over at Francesca Del Ray, who was examining her nails.

She lifted her eyes and smiled. "I think Dr. Cole is expendable, Sir Richard," she said in a whisper.

"Well, then, Melchior, you see to the spiritual powers, and I will see to the physical. Together, the Intergalactic Council will not be able to stand against us. I will defeat their ships, and you will cloud their minds."

"So be it then, Sir Richard."

Sir Richard turned from the console. "Well, my dear, things appear to be coming together. How would you like being Empress of the Galaxy?"

"I would like it very much indeed." Then she frowned. "I don't trust that woman. Better to eliminate her at once."

"I believe Melchior and Iona will be able to handle her. If she were destroyed now, it might cause Edge to wake up to the truth, and that is the last thing we want."

On far-off Merlina, the Chief Wizard and Iona were having their own conversation.

Iona said, "Sir Richard Irons is a strong man."

"Yes, in one sense," Melchior agreed, "but he is a fool in other ways. We can use him."

Iona's smile was cruel. "He is used to using others. He would not dream that anyone would be strong enough to use him."

They exchanged smiles, and then Iona laughed. "What fools people are to think they can stand against the forces of darkness without defense!"

"I think it is time to take the next step," Melchior said.

"And what is that?"

"We will cause Edge to bring the *Daystar* within range of the city. We already know that there are Christians aboard, and we must overcome them before we can carry out our designs with the captain."

"Even he may be troublesome. I have spoken with the woman. She says he's very fond of those he calls the Junior Space Rangers. They are very young, but most of them are believers. Perhaps it would be better to simply kill them all."

"I think not, my dear. That would certainly not win over Captain Edge. We must simply cloud his mind so that he will be our slave. Then he will carry back any message we choose to send to Commandant Lee. Have you been enjoying success with our good Captain Edge?"

"Oh, yes. I have already begun to cast a spell over him. And he has not the least idea of this, of course."

"Good. We will command him to bring the ship to Merlina at once."

Heck Jordan was working with a complicated bit of equipment. After melting holes in three different circuit board pathways, he threw his hands into the air and screamed. He looked at the damaged system and put down his tools. "I don't know what's wrong with me. I can't seem to do anything right today."

It was an admission that Jordan would never make to anyone else. He glanced over at Ivan Petroski, who had entered through the portal, and quickly said, "Almost through, Chief."

Petroski came over and scrutinized the work. He ran his hands over the circuits and read the computer monitor. "It's still not fixed, Jordan. What's wrong with you?"

"I'm bored—that's what's wrong! Are we gonna sit out here in the wilderness forever? When is the captain coming back?"

At that moment Zeno Thrax entered through another portal. "We've just received a radio message," he said. "The captain is on his way back."

"Well!" Heck exclaimed. "*Now* maybe we can get something done!" He pulled a box of sweets out of his pocket, then popped one into his mouth. Sucking on it noisily, he said, "I've got an idea for the three of us. I think we ought to go into business together."

Thrax glanced at the boy. "Your scheme would never work. It would not be honest."

Heck blinked, then got up, exploding, "Well, I didn't know I was dealing with such religious people!" He stalked off angrily.

Petroski raised his eyebrows. "What did he have on his mind, Zeno?"

"Oh, a new scheme to bilk the Merlinians out of what belongs to them. That's a very troubled young man. He always wants *more*. He's going to run into difficulty some day."

Ivan drew himself up to his full four feet six. "I guess we all want more," he said. "I'd like to get enough together to go back to Bellinka rich as a king."

Zeno smiled faintly. "I wish you good fortune, Ivan."

"Wouldn't you like to be rich, Zeno?"

"No. I haven't noticed that being rich brings any happiness."

"I keep thinking about that tridium on Makon. If we could just get back there. As the captain says, we'd all be rich."

"And I'm not sure that would be a good thing."

Ivan Petroski wasn't as perceptive as Zeno Thrax, but he was an intelligent man. He turned his sharp eyes on the albino and said, "You know what I think? I think you've been listening to these Christians. I heard that sermon that Raina St. Clair preached yesterday. It was mostly about money and how little happiness it brings."

"I thought it was a very wise address. If you just look around, Ivan, you'll see that people that have money are not particularly happier than people who don't."

But Ivan Petroski said, "I think I'll go talk to Heck. Maybe he and I can go into business together after all."

When the dwarf left, Zeno walked on through the ship, stopping from time to time to check its many circuits. The *Daystar* had become home to him. He knew every bolt, every circuit, every facet of it.

When he came to where Tara Jaleel was sitting

with Studs Cagney, he gave them his message. "The captain's returning."

"Good," Studs said. "I want to get out of this place. It doesn't feel good to me."

Tara Jaleel frowned at him, her features caught by the light of the overhead lamp that cast shadows over her eyes. "What does that mean—'it doesn't feel good'?"

"You know what they say about this place. Everybody knows there's magicians around here. I'd just as soon leave today."

Jaleel shook her head. "You're just superstitious."

"I'm smart is what I am."

"Well, I'll go tell the rest of the crew," Zeno remarked. "We need to be ready for the captain's return."

He found Jerusha, Mei-Lani, and Raina in the lounge and made his announcement. "I think we will see some action now," he told them.

Mei-Lani seemed depressed. "I've been studying more about Merlina, and it's not good," she said. "This place is filled with demon worshipers. They even practice human sacrifice."

"I'd still feel better if the captain had taken one of us along," Jerusha murmured.

"I agree." Raina ran a hand over her hair.

"We need to be sure the ship is in first class order before the captain returns," Zeno said.

"All right." Raina got to her feet. "Let's get at it."

"They're here!" Ringo Smith had been at the porthole when two figures emerged from the foliage. "It's the doctor and the captain," he announced.

Jerusha and the other Junior Space Rangers piled out of the *Daystar* and formed a line along with other members of the crew.

As soon as they were close enough, Edge called, "Hello! All ready to greet your captain, I see."

"It's good to have you back, Captain Edge," Zeno said. He shook the captain's hand. "Was your mission successful?"

"Very much so. Let's go inside, and I'll give you a report."

When the officers and ensigns were gathered around the white enamel table in the war room, Edge greeted each one. "Has everything been going well with the ship?"

"Very well, Captain," Tara Jaleel said, leaning forward. "The weapons systems are in first-class condition. We're ready for any kind of strike that you might order."

"There'll be no strike," Edge said. He turned to the woman beside him. "We had a successful mission indeed, didn't we, Doctor?"

"I was very happy, and I think you all will be, too."

The captain smiled fondly at the doctor, and Jerusha felt her anger stirring. "What did the wizards say, Captain?"

"They're not like the wizards that you're afraid of—wizards who use black magic and demons and all of that," Edge said. "They're very intelligent people and most hospitable. We looked over the whole city and saw no signs of slavery."

Jerusha said, "But what about Rowdan and his people? He tells us that all over the planet there are bands like his that are being gradually overcome."

"I'm afraid Rowdan's been misinformed and misled," Edge said. He explained what the wizards had told them—that there were indeed certain discontented people on the planet. "But all Rowdan and his peo-

131

ple have to do is to give themselves up, and all will be well."

Raina St. Clair leaned over and whispered urgently, "Jerusha, something's terribly *wrong* with Captain Edge!"

"Very wrong." Jerusha thought she had learned to understand Mark Edge, but now she found herself baffled. "Raina," she breathed, "that's not the captain we knew. He's so changed. I don't know how to say it, but it's like . . . it's like he's under a . . . spell."

Mei-Lani, sitting close enough to hear, murmured, "He *is* different. Something has happened."

After the meeting Raina told Jerusha and Mei-Lani, "We must get all the Rangers together. We've got to do something." And late that night, when all the ship was asleep, the ensigns met.

"We hate to tell you this," Raina said, "but something is wrong with the captain."

Jerusha put in, "He's not himself. All you have to do is look at him to see that."

Heck stared at his companions. "I don't see anything the matter with him. It all sounds great to me."

Mei-Lani spoke up. "Do you think the captain's lying to us, Jerusha? Did you pick up on that?"

Jerusha shook her head sadly. "No, it's not that he's lying. He *thinks* he's telling the truth—but he's not."

Dai Bando was puzzled by all of this. "What do you think is happening?"

"I think he's controlled," Jerusha said, her face drawn tight.

Dai stared at her. "You mean like somebody's put a spell on him?"

"That's exactly what I mean, Dai! He's not himself at all. Just look into his eyes. He smiles, but it doesn't reach as far as his eyes. Something happened to him in that place—and I think Dr. Temple Cole is responsible for it." Then Jerusha added, "And did you notice how Contessa reacted to him?"

"No. What did she do?" Ringo asked.

"The hair on her back stood up. And you know how she loves Captain Edge, but what she sees now frightens her and makes her angry. Even *she* knows something's wrong."

"What are we going to do about it?" Mei-Lani asked.

Raina St. Clair said, "There's only one thing we can do. He's our captain, and we're under his orders. If he's not himself, then we'll have to pray for him. We'll have to pray until the old Captain Edge comes back."

13
The Wizards Strike

Sleep would not come for Raina St. Clair. She tossed and turned and finally in despair got up and dressed. A pale dawn was lightening the horizon, and she felt the morning chill as she left the *Daystar* and began walking. Far overhead a few brilliant stars still glittered like diamonds, and the landscape shimmered as the light began to dispel the darkness.

For more than an hour she walked among the trees, struggling with the problem. She felt alone. She felt as though her prayers did not get any higher than the leafy foliage that from time to time blotted out the dimming stars.

"Oh, God, hear me!" she prayed aloud in desperation. She fell to her knees and began to pray both aloud and silently. "We must have Your help—Your guidance!" A long time passed, and despair seized her heart like a cold fist.

Suddenly, something cold touched the back of her neck. Startled, she whirled to find Contessa standing there, her tail down and a whine in her throat. Throwing her arms around the huge German shepherd, Raina knelt with tears running down her cheeks. "Oh, Contessa . . ."

Whining a high-pitched growl, Contessa tried to lick the tears from the girl's face. She pawed at her with a huge forepaw and seemed to be saying, "I'd like to help if I could."

Raina kept an arm around the heavily muscled

shoulders of the dog, and Contessa pressed as close to her as she could. Raina continued to pray.

And as the sun began to come up, even as she was about to give up all hope of receiving some direction from God, something came to Raina's mind. It was not a spoken word—she could not even identify words—but the impression was as plain as if it had been printed out on a white page in bold black letters: *You must go to Captain Edge and pray for him.*

Raina uttered a glad cry. "Thank you, Lord!"

She jumped to her feet and ran back toward the *Daystar.* Contessa, seeming to sense a difference in the girl, barked happily and galloped alongside.

When they reached the cruiser, Raina found the captain already standing on the bridge, his eyes fixed on the computer.

"Captain Edge, I must see you."

"What is it?" Edge said. He turned, and again she saw the emptiness in his eyes. Contessa growled deep in her throat and lowered her head, and the captain said, "Get that animal off the bridge."

"Contessa, be quiet." Raina said, "Please, Captain, could I see you alone?"

"Say what you have to say, Ensign."

This was a different Mark Edge than Raina had ever seen. Before, his eyes had always been keen, his mind sharp and quick, but now there was an indifference about him.

He stood waiting, and her heart sank. *Oh, God, I don't know how to handle this.*

Pray for him!

Once again the impression was as clear to Raina as if it had been shouted.

"Almighty God, in the name of Jesus I ask that You touch my captain. Help him to—"

"Leave the bridge!" Edge's face had gone pale. A frantic look came into his eyes. Even his voice sounded harsh and different. "I'll have none of that!"

"But, Captain—"

"Did you hear me, Ensign? I order you to leave the bridge!"

Raina turned away and whispered, "Come, Contessa."

Her shoulders drooped as she left the bridge. *Oh, God, I've failed! I couldn't do what You asked.*

Yet there was no sense of having displeased Him, and although it appeared that she had not accomplished anything, she felt a strange peace. It was as if a voice whispered, "You have been obedient, My daughter. Peace be upon you."

Jerusha Ericson had tossed all night. She'd gotten up several times to sit in a chair and stare blindly at the bulkhead. Emotions swept across her mind—confusion, anger, grief. Since Jerusha prided herself on her steadiness of mind, this was a terrible experience. More than once during that long night she had to fight back tears, for she felt in the grip of a situation that she could not control.

And then she heard a bark outside her door.

Jerusha opened it to find Raina and Contessa standing there. The dog at once leaped inside and placed her paws on Jerusha's shoulders.

"Get down, Contessa." She glanced at Raina and saw dark shadows like smudges under the girl's eyes. "You couldn't sleep either."

"No. I went out to pray." Raina told Jerusha of her experience. "I tried to do what seemed right, but I don't know what good it did. He wouldn't let me pray for him."

"We've got to do something!" Jerusha exclaimed. "The captain's doomed if we don't—and so are we, perhaps."

"I've the feeling that these wizards would like nothing better than to destroy all the Christians on this ship. But what can we do?"

They talked in whispers, as though they might be overheard. And then Jerusha took a deep breath. "Maybe we ought to go talk to Dr. Cole."

Raina studied the features of her friend. "You still think she's responsible for what's happened to the captain?"

"I do. There's something in her that isn't good. Will you come with me?"

Raina hesitated. "Perhaps it would be better if I waited here with Contessa and prayed for you. If both of us go, she might get even more defensive."

"All right, then. I'll go. Pray for me before I leave, Raina."

Raina put her hands on her friend's shoulders and prayed fervently that Jerusha would be clothed in full spiritual armor.

Then Jerusha walked with determination down the corridor. She considered going to talk to Bronwen Llewellen first, but there was little time. "The captain will be moving the ship into Merlina City soon," she muttered, "and it may be too late then."

Reaching the doctor's cabin, she touched the button.

"Yes? Who is it?"

"Ensign Ericson, Doctor."

After a hesitation, the voice said, "All right. Come in."

Dr. Cole was seated at her desk. Her strawberry blonde hair was tied up in a neat coil on the back of her head. Her eyes were wary. "What is it, Ensign? Are you ill?"

Now that Jerusha was there she did not know what to say. Desperately she tried to read the emotions of the woman, but all she picked up was a confused signal.

Something was there, though, that had not been there before. Previously when she had tried to understand the doctor, she had met nothing but a blank wall. Now, however, she sensed—fear? This came as a surprise and a shock to Jerusha. She swallowed hard, then said, "Dr. Cole, I want to talk to you about the captain."

"What about him?"

"You must know that he's not himself."

"He seems to be in full control. I don't know what you mean."

"I think you do. I haven't known you very long, Dr. Cole, but I want to appeal to your integrity."

"I don't know what you're talking about! Are you ill, Ensign? Do you need medical attention?"

"I don't, but the captain does. He's influenced by . . . something. Surely you must see that."

Temple Cole's eyes looked decidedly apprehensive. But she stood listening as Jerusha pleaded with her to help restore the captain. Then she said abruptly, "You're mistaken. The captain is as he always was."

"Dr. Cole, you are an unhappy woman."

The surgeon's eyes opened wide as if she had heard something that struck her hard. "Leave my cabin, Ensign!"

Jerusha felt helpless to penetrate the wall that Temple Cole had built around herself, and she was convinced that this woman would do exactly what she had set out to do. But she tried once more. "Sometimes, Doctor," she said, "we come to a fork in the road. If we take one fork, it leads to ruin. If we take another, it leads to happiness. I think"—Jerusha's eyes were fixed full on the doctor—"you're at that fork in the road now."

"Get out of my cabin!" Dr. Cole actually reached forward, turned Jerusha around, and shoved her out the door. But then she pushed past her and went, almost at a run, toward the bridge.

As Temple Cole hurried toward the lift, a sudden thought came to her. It was more a picture than a thought of words. She remembered herself about to die, and then Mark Edge throwing himself on the scaly serpent, risking his life for her. The image was so sharp she almost could smell the stench of the monster.

The doctor caught her breath and stood still in the passageway, reliving the moment. Her emotions, which she had tried to keep under firm control, were suddenly loosed, and something seemed to say, *Don't do this thing!*

But I've got to. Dr. Cole knew she was indeed poised at a fork in the road such as Jerusha Ericson had mentioned. But she steeled herself and shut out the warning voice. Placing her hands over her ears, she whispered, "I can't help myself! I've *got* to get what I want!" With a sob she continued toward the bridge.

Captain Edge greeted her in a rather strained voice. "Time to go to Merlina. The wizards will be waiting."

"Yes, Captain. We must go to the wizards."

Dr. Cole stood by as Edge gave the order to activate the ship. Something cold seemed to enclose her. She tried to ignore it, but it was like a horrible breath from the grave. Mark Edge's eyes frightened her. As the ship came to life and the takeoff was initiated, she began to tremble.

"I'm *afraid* of this place."

Heck Jordan looked over at Ringo and bobbed his head. "I don't like it much myself."

With the *Daystar* crew, Heck and Ringo had been escorted to the High Tower. They were all now standing in front of the wizards, who sat behind a table. A few guards were in the room, but they seemed to carry no weapons. The crew's own weapons had been taken from them, so now they waited, quite helpless.

"I don't like the looks of this Melchior," Heck murmured nervously. He rubbed his forehead. "And that Iona. She's a bad one!"

Ringo agreed completely but could not answer. He felt trapped. The evil atmosphere in the room was so thick it could almost be cut with a knife. He had sensed something about Merlina City as soon as they entered the place, and now that they were in the heart of the wizards' High Council, it seemed to grip him like a cold iron fist.

Ringo turned his head slightly to glance at Dai Bando, standing on his left. The tall boy was gazing at the wizards, and there was a tense expression on his smooth face. This was unusual for Dai. "What do you think?" Ringo whispered.

"This is not a good place."

Ringo wanted to ask more, but the Chief Wizard was getting up. He wore white trimmed in silver, and his silver hair seemed to glow. But it was his eyes that frightened Ringo. Somehow the boy knew that something awful was hidden in those gray eyes, colder than polar ice. He swallowed hard and felt a trembling in his limbs that he tried to control.

"Well, Captain Edge, you have brought your entire crew, I see."

"Yes, Melchior."

Melchior smiled at the obedient reply. His eyes turned then to the young people, who stood grouped together. One by one he studied them, and when his eyes met Ringo's, something like a sharp knife seemed to slide into the young man's mind.

Panic shot through Ringo. It was as if he were inside a room and a horrible beast was trying to open the door to get at him. Somehow he knew that once he let the beast inside, he was lost. He wondered if the other ensigns were experiencing the same thing. Shutting his eyes, Ringo began to silently pray.

Heck seemed to see himself running from giant dark beasts with razor-sharp claws. No matter how fast he ran, they gained on him. Finally, the nightmarish creatures cornered him, ready for the kill. "Yield to us or die," they shrieked.

Heck suddenly sat on the floor and covered his head with his arms.

Raina dropped down beside him and put her arms around him. She began to pray.

The sorceress came to her feet. "Silence that girl!"

Heck looked up. There was no physical movement toward Raina, but the eyes of all the wizards were fixed on her. And he sensed a terrible barrage of evil.

Bronwen Llewellen came to stand over the two young people, then. She began to speak aloud in a language that Heck suspected was Welsh. He was sure she was praying.

Iona, the sorceress, threw her hands over her ears and screamed, "Stop that woman!"

Now it was Bronwen who took the full barrage of

the wizards' evil powers. She grew pale, and her voice dropped to a whisper. She seemed about to fall.

Mei-Lani Lao cried, "They are trying to control us! All believers in the Lord Jesus Christ, come together!" And Mei-Lani, Dai, and Jerusha joined the little group facing the wizards.

Captain Edge, who had stood watching, suddenly shouted, "No!"

But the sorceress turned on him, and her eyes glittered. "Quiet! You are not one of them! You are one of us!"

Temple Cole could not move. She stood helpless as the scene unfolded, feeling that she would be sick! *I can't stand any more of this!* she thought miserably.

Temple's face was white as paste. She trembled as she saw what was happening, knowing that it was all her doing. She felt the urge to throw herself at the captain and call for him to come out of whatever prison he had been put in by the wizards of Merlina.

But she did not. One burning look from Melchior held her in place. Shuddering, she watched the struggle between the wizards and the ensigns continue.

One by one, the ensigns collapsed. Ringo Smith went down, falling beside Heck, who now seemed to be unconscious. Jerusha, almost falling, was able to say in a loud, clear voice, "In the name of Jesus Christ of Nazareth, I command you to—"

But she got no farther, for Melchior screamed, "Powers of darkness, fall upon them!"

Instantly all the wizards and the sorceress descended upon the small group. The room almost crackled with the intensity of the struggle.

"Throw them all in the dungeon!" the Chief Wizard cried. "We will deal with them later—publicly."

Temple Cole watched the guards gather up the defenseless young people. As she saw one large guard carry Raina's limp body from the room, Temple knew that indeed something terrible was happening.

And it's all my fault. I did all this, she thought desperately.

Then she saw that the sorceress, Iona, in her silver gown with the sign of the broken cross emblazoned on her bosom, was looking at her with a peculiar expression.

Iona approached the doctor. Her eyes were hard, but her voice was silky as she said, "You must become wholly one with us, Doctor. You must not fight against us."

Helplessly, Temple felt herself falling under the power of the sorceress. She struggled, but a gray haze began to swirl about her, then close in. She heard herself cry out, "Oh, no!" as darkness descended like a deadly curtain.

14

A Light in a Dark Place

A contented smile curled the lips of Iona, the sorceress. She was sitting with Melchior in their chambers, which were decked with emblems of the broken cross. "I believe we have solved our problem."

Melchior returned her smile. "Yes, and I have just finished speaking with Sir Richard Irons."

"And what did Sir Richard say?"

The Chief Wizard's eyes gleamed. "About what I imagined he would say." He poured himself a goblet of dark red wine, drank it off, and laughed aloud. "Sir Richard commands that we execute all of the Christians."

"Sir Richard *commands*." The sorceress joined in his laughter. "The fool! He does not understand that soon he will not command anyone. He will be in our power."

"Yes, we almost have him now. As soon as we dispense with these Junior Space Rangers—and the others on the crew who call themselves . . ." This time he seemed unable to pronounce the word he intended to say, and his eyes hardened. "In any case, we will be obedient to Sir Richard so far as that part is concerned."

"What else did he have to say?"

"Oh, he was very insistent that Captain Edge be preserved alive." He poured another glassful of the wine and swirled it in the goblet. "He intends to make himself rich by the tridium Captain Edge has found on Makon."

"I imagine we could get the location of the planet Makon from the captain."

"When we turn him over to the torturers, he will wish he had more to tell us."

"When will the executions be?"

"As soon as they can be carried out publicly. There are still rebels who think to overthrow our government. When they see how hopeless they are in our hands, I think that will be the end of their little revolution."

"I will try to think of something interesting by way of putting the Christians out of this world." Anger seemed to sweep over her then. "If they love their Christ so much, we will properly send them to meet Him."

The two smiled at each other, but there was no humor in their expressions. They began making plans for the executions to come.

The dungeon was deep underground. The ensigns and their friends had been hustled down stone steps carved into the bowels of the planet. The way had been lighted only faintly as the guards half carried, half shoved them downward. The farther they went, the more awful the place became. More than once they passed by doors where from tiny barred grills emitted cries of pain, and there was a hopeless quality to the voices that cried out from inside those cells.

The guards stopped before a door and shoved them inside, one by one.

Ringo fell, and his head struck the stone floor. He looked up into the jeering eyes of one of the guards, who said, "Enjoy yourself." The man winked at one of his companions. "I don't think he'll be enjoying our hospitality too long."

"That's right." The other guard laughed harshly. "I expect there'll be fine sport with you tender young things."

The first guard said, "Let me tell you about some of the other executions the sorceress has arranged." He began to speak of awful things, horrible things— how Christians captured by the wizards had been put to death in unspeakable ways.

Ringo was afraid, but he was determined to show nothing. He stood and met the guard's eyes fully.

This seemed to anger the man. He barked, "Come on! Let's see how they like their last few hours of life!"

The door clanged shut, and Ringo looked around to see that the others seemed to be as troubled as he. The cell itself was merely a large rectangle with a few straw mattresses thrown carelessly about. There was an awful smell to the place, and the dim light seemed to harden the features of his fellow prisoners.

Dai Bando walked around, looking over the cell. "Not a very pretty place, is it?" he murmured, but he did not seem to be afraid. He put a hand on Bronwen's shoulder and said, "Are you all right, Aunt?"

"I'm all right now, Dai."

But Ringo knew that the struggle in the High Tower had taken something out of Bronwen Llewellen. She showed her age now and was trembling.

"The battle against those evil wizards—it was awful," she whispered.

"Come. Lie down. You'll feel better after while," Dai said gently. He sat beside her on one of the straw mats and held her hand. "Are you all right, Raina?"

"I—I'm not sure." Raina still looked confused from the terrible power of evil that had been thrown against her. But she brushed a hand across her face as if removing a veil, and then a determined look came into her green eyes. "Yes, I'm all right, Dai."

Heck Jordan had returned to consciousness. "What's going to happen to us?" he asked. He sat against the wall and drew up his legs in a defensive position. "How are we going to get out of here?"

"I don't think we are," Ringo muttered.

Heck said, "If given the choice of execution or dying at the hands of those dark beasts I saw—I'll pick execution any day! You have no idea how terrifying they are!"

"I don't think you have to worry," Ringo said. "They're going to execute us."

Despite himself, his voice trembled, and Raina came to him and took his hand, smiling but saying nothing. Her touch seemed to help, though, and Ringo whispered his thanks.

Mei-Lani, the youngest of them all, was able to hide her feelings behind her smooth face. She knew, better than the others, about the terrible things that the wizards could do to them. She had studied their history. Now fear tried to rise in her as she thought about how brief her life had been. She had wisdom beyond her years, however, and knew that fear could destroy as quickly as a Neuromag.

"I think," she said, "that we had better encourage one another."

Raina lifted her head, and Jerusha also seemed to come alive.

"How shall we do that, Mei-Lani?" Jerusha asked.

Mei-Lani thought for a moment. "Do you remember what happened in the book of Acts, the sixteenth chapter?"

"Yes. I remember." Raina smiled.

"What's that all about?" Heck muttered. He looked terrible.

Mei-Lani went over and sat beside him, taking his hand. "In the Bible, Paul and Silas were thrown into a prison. About like this one, I suppose."

Dai said, "You told me that story before I could even read, Aunt."

Bronwen Llewellen seemed to be growing somewhat stronger. She sat up and looked around at their prison, then nodded at Heck. "All prisons are about the same, but if God is in the prison with you, then it's not a prison after all."

Heck stared at her. "I don't care what any of you say. I'm scared, and I don't care who knows it."

Ringo swallowed. "So am I."

"I'm afraid, too," Mei-Lani said, "but the Bible says that God has not given us the spirit of fear but of power and love and a sound mind."

"Well, I'm not going to have a sound mind. I'm going crazy if we don't get out of here!" Heck protested, shivering. "Did you hear what that guard said they're going to do to us?"

"It's not done yet, Heck," Dai spoke up strongly. "Tell him what happened to Paul and Silas in their prison, Mei-Lani."

Mei-Lani had no Bible, but she knew the words by heart. She began to quote slowly, "'The crowd rose up together against them, and the chief magistrates tore their robes off them, and proceeded to order them to be beaten with rods.'"

Mei-Lani looked from face to face as she spoke. "'When they had struck them with many blows, they threw them into prison, commanding the jailer to guard them securely; and he, having received such a

149

command, threw them into the inner prison and fastened their feet in the stocks.'"

She continued, "'But about midnight Paul and Silas were praying and singing hymns of praise to God, and the prisoners were listening to them; and suddenly there came a great earthquake, so that the foundations of the prison house were shaken; and immediately all the doors were opened and everyone's chains were unfastened.'"

When Mei-Lani paused, Jerusha went over to Heck and put an arm around his shoulders.

He looked up at her, startled. She had never done such a thing before.

"We must trust God, Heck," she said quietly. "He is far more powerful than all the dark powers put together."

Heck dropped his eyes. "I don't know God. And I'm nothing but a wimp!"

Jerusha smiled. "We're all wimps in one way or another, but Jesus loves us anyway. He died for wimps."

Mei-Lani's words seemed to have a soothing effect on all of them. When she was finished, Ringo said shakily, "That's a wonderful story, Mei-Lani."

"All that God does is wonderful," she said. "But now we must do our part."

Raina seemed to know exactly what Mei-Lani was talking about. "Yes," she said instantly. "So many times in the Bible, when God's people fell into hard circumstances, they had to do their part."

"So what is our part?" Ringo asked.

"Fasting and prayer." Bronwen Llewellen spoke up from where she sat next to Dai. A smile lit her eyes. "We don't have to worry about the fasting, but what we need to do now is to pray."

Ringo lowered his head and stared at the cold

stone pavement. "I don't think I can pray much," he said. "I'm not much of a pray-er."

"It's good you feel like that." Raina smiled at him. "If you had said, 'Well, I can handle this. I'm a great prayer warrior,' it would have been hopeless. But God hears the humble and the broken in spirit, and that's what we must become. Jesus Christ is alive and able to save us, if He wants to. We must give ourselves completely to Him."

"You mean He might not *want* to?" Heck asked in alarm.

"Sometimes He has other plans," Raina answered. "Many believers have died for their faith. Mei-Lani knows church history. She could tell you about those who have died trusting God."

"Better to die trusting in God than to live not trusting Him," Dai said. "And also sometimes people prayed for days before God rescued them."

"We may not have days!" Ringo protested.

"Well, we'll take what time we do have," Mei-Lani said. "We may not be able to see God or hear His voice, but He's here all the same. Now, I'm going to pray that He will somehow get glory out of our being in this dungeon."

Mei-Lani knelt and began to pray, her voice almost inaudible.

Ringo watched others kneel and begin to pray. Then he himself bowed his head. The words came hard, but he finally managed to stammer, "God, I'm not much of a one to pray. I just haven't prayed the way I should have. But I'm with praying folks here. And I'm asking You to please help us in this mess!"

None of the ensigns wore a watch so had no way

of knowing what time it was. But many long, weary hours seemed to pass. Once, the guards had come and left a little food and water, but none of them touched the food. They only drank thirstily. They were, indeed, fasting.

It was Dai who said wryly, "It's not hard to fast when all they offer you to eat is garbage."

Time seemed to drag especially for Ringo. To him it felt that days had passed in the murky gloom of the dungeon. More than once he wanted to scream, "It's no good! Prayer isn't going to work!" But repeatedly he had been encouraged by Raina, who seemed to know he was having a hard time.

Heck had simply given up. He managed to fall asleep.

From time to time the others took small troubled naps, and then they would awake and begin to pray again.

When the guards had brought water and food twice more, Ringo whispered hoarsely, "It's no good, Raina. No good. I just can't *feel* God in here."

"What you feel doesn't matter," she whispered back.

"We're going to die, and I'm scared stiff!"

"I'm going to pray for you. We've all got to pray for one another."

Ringo listened to Raina praying for him, and it encouraged him for a time. But later he felt overwhelmed again and threw himself down on one of the filthy mattresses. Finally he drifted off to sleep, grateful to be out of the world that had turned so cruel.

A voice was calling, and Ringo did not want to come out of his warm blanket of sleep. It called again, soft and insistent. It called his name.

"Go away," he muttered, but the voice persisted.

152

Slowly Ringo opened his eyes and was shocked when he saw that there was an addition to their number. A man stood by him dressed in a simple robe. It seemed to be white, but at times it also seemed to have colors that flashed and glowed as he moved. His face was half hidden by a cowl, but Ringo could see the man's bright eyes studying him.

"Who are you?" he whispered, coming to a sitting position with his back pressed against the wall. There was a trembling in his legs and his hands that he could not control.

"One sent to help you."

Ringo could not think clearly. He leaned forward and tried to see the features of the man. He saw only that there was a kind expression on his face and that his features were sharply defined underneath the cowl. Again he asked, "Who are you?"

"My name is not important. What is important is that you believe what I am about to say." The voice was soft and yet at the same time powerful. Ringo had the idea that if the man raised his voice, he could shake the very stones of the prison.

He saw that the others were still sleeping. "Is this a dream?"

"Call it what you wish—a dream or a vision or a reality. It doesn't matter. Again, what matters is that you believe what I am going to say."

Strangely, the dungeon seemed less dark. It was as if light emanated from the cloak of the strange being and lit up this dark place.

"What is it you want me to believe?"

"You must believe that God knows your pain and your fears."

Ringo blinked with surprise. Then he swallowed hard. "I'll try, but it's hard when you're facing . . ."

"I know, but it is important," the voice went on steadily, "that you believe that God cares. He says He does. Can you believe Him?"

Ringo could not for the life of him tell if he was having a dream or if some sort of visitor had actually come into the dungeon. He knew one thing—the visitor was not one of the wizards. There was a goodness and a love in the man's strong features that made that impossible.

"Are you an . . . an angel?" he whispered in a voice that was not steady.

"Do not ask who I am or my name. I am simply sent to tell you that you will not perish in this place. Can you believe that?"

Ringo found his throat tightening, and tears came to his eyes. "If you say so, sir."

"Then you must tell your companions. Be strong and of good courage. Your God has not forgotten you, Ringo Smith."

Ringo was never sure what happened next. The man was there, then he faded away. And Ringo found himself lying on the filthy straw mattress instead of sitting up. He opened his eyes and looked around wildly for the visitor—but there was nothing!

"It was all a dream," Ringo spoke aloud in disappointment.

"What did you say, Ringo?"

Raina, who'd been lying on another mat nearby, struggled to sit up. "What did you say?" she asked again.

Ringo almost said, "Nothing," but then he remembered the words of the visitor: *You must tell your companions.*

"You'll think I'm crazy, but something just happened." Raina was staring at him in a strange way, and he knew that he might well be making a fool of himself.

"Is it something we all need to hear?" she asked quietly.

"I—I think so."

"Everyone! Wake up! Something's happened to Ringo."

The others began to stir. Finally all were standing, and he stood with them. Then he found he could not say a word.

Raina seemed to understand his confusion. "Whatever it is, Ringo, go ahead and say it. We're all brothers and sisters here."

Her words encouraged him. He swallowed hard and said, "Well, this sounds crazy, but I think I had a dream. I don't dream much, but this was so real . . ."

"What was your dream?" Bronwen Llewellen asked.

"Well, I dreamed that this man was here. He was wearing some sort of robe and a cover over his head. His robe seemed to glow, and it—it lit up the whole cell." Ringo stammered slightly, and he looked around, half expecting the others to laugh. But there was no mockery in anyone's eyes.

Dai Bando leaned toward him. "What did he look like?"

"I don't know, Dai. I couldn't see him clearly, and his voice—well, it was different from anybody's voice I've ever heard."

"What did he say, Ringo?" Mei-Lani asked eagerly.

"All he said was that I was to believe that God knew about our troubles, and then he said he'd been sent to tell us that we weren't going to die in this dungeon."

"Praise be to the Lord!" Bronwen exclaimed, and a joyous light came into her eyes. "Our God is a great God, and no one can save like Him!"

Heck stared at her. "Does this mean we're going to be all right, or was it just a dream?"

"I don't have dreams like this, Heck. As a matter of fact, I don't dream much at all." Ringo thought about his visitor. "No, I don't think I could dream about anyone like this."

"It must have been an angel," Jerusha said quietly. She put an arm around Mei-Lani and hugged her. "Do you think so, Mei-Lani?"

Mei-Lani's eyes glowed, and her voice was full of faith. "I believe God has sent His angel to give us a message of hope."

Ringo shifted uncertainly. "I don't know," he said. "I mean, why would he come to me? I'm the worst of the lot."

Bronwen Llewellen said, "God chooses whom He pleases, and He loves to use weak instruments to do His will."

Then Ringo Smith, tired and shaken by fears and worn to the point of exhaustion, said, "Well, if He was looking for a weak instrument, He found one in me!"

15

The Rescue

A strange and peaceful silence had fallen over the dungeon where the Junior Space Rangers were confined. After Ringo's telling of his visitor, somehow faith was strengthened in each one of them.

Except, that is, for Heck Jordan, who still was terrified of the ordeal that lay ahead. Jerusha and especially Raina stayed close and tried to encourage him, but he merely shook his head and kept his eyes closed.

When the girls had moved off to a far corner of the dungeon, Raina said with sadness in her voice, "He's defenseless. Since he doesn't know the Lord, he can't count on the Lord to give him protection."

"I know," Jerusha answered in a whisper. She looked back across the room. Everyone else was quiet. Most were sitting still, their eyes closed, although Dai Bando was curled up, sleeping.

Suddenly, Ringo jumped up. "They're coming!"

Immediately all except for Heck came to their feet.

"I don't hear anything," Jerusha said.

Raina touched Ringo on the arm. "It's that super hearing of yours, isn't it?"

Ringo had no time to answer, for the door opened, and the light that suddenly flooded the place was blinding. There had been no illumination in the dungeon except one small murky lamp, and they had to cover their eyes until they adjusted.

"It is time," the guard said. He was new, Jerusha

noted—a tall man with steely eyes and dressed entirely in black. He watched them carefully. "Do you understand? It is time for your execution."

Mei-Lani answered for them all. "If this is what God has for us, we are ready."

The guard stepped back as though in shock. Probably he had done this many times, always enjoying the fear that came over the victims. "I am the chief executioner," he announced. Then he said loudly, "I will have you carried if you are unable to walk."

"That will not be necessary," Raina said. She reached down and touched Heck, who got to his feet.

The guard's eyes fell on him, and he laughed. "*That* one will need to be carried!"

"No, he won't," Raina said firmly. "Come, Heck. Put your trust in the Lord Jesus."

The words seemed to inflame the guard. He shouted, "Out of here! All of you! Your Jesus is going to let you die today!"

"Blessed are the dead that die in the Lord." Bronwen stepped forward, small, frail, with silver hair, her face drawn. But there was a look of peace in her fine eyes. "We are ready for whatever God has for us."

Her words seemed to anger the executioner once again. He snarled, "Bring them along! If they loiter, you know what to do!"

Bronwen and the young people followed him. Dai Bando was walking beside Mei-Lani, who reached out and took his hand. He smiled down at her and then turned to look at his aunt. "Are you all right, Aunt?"

"Resting in the Lord," Bronwen said. "If it is the Lord's will, we will soon be in the presence of our God—and that is the best thing that can happen to any Christian."

Ringo and Raina found themselves walking together.

"I'm still afraid," Ringo said, "but not like I was."

Raina smiled at him brilliantly. "I'm glad you're here. I feel better with you by my side."

"Do you really?"

"Why, of course. You know how much I've always liked you, Ringo."

Ringo said nothing for a while, then finally he murmured, "No, I didn't know that."

Jerusha and Heck brought up the rear. She kept her hand on Heck's arm.

The ensigns and Bronwen Llewellen were taken up a flight of narrow, dank steps, and their footsteps made hollow echoes as they ascended. When they reached an upper level, a door opened, and the executioner said, "We have a fine crowd today. I've never seen so many people come out for an execution. Now, come this way."

By this time Jerusha's eyes had become accustomed to brighter light. However, now once again she had to blink. They had stepped into an arena, an enormous, round, open field surrounded by what appeared to be thousands of people.

Jerusha quickly sensed the mood of the crowd. She thought, *There's a lot of hatred and darkness here, but it's not all hatred and darkness.* She turned to Heck. "Be of good cheer, Heck. God is on our side."

Heck took a deep breath and said in a voice that trembled, "It doesn't look like it. It looks like there's thousands of them and only a handful of us."

"But God is not on the side of the biggest crowd."

Hearing Jerusha's remark, Raina looked back and smiled. "That's right, Heck. One of us with God is more than the whole world drawn up against us."

"Over there!"

The prisoners were hustled forward by the jeering attendants. One of them, a short, fat man with a cruel mouth, shoved Jerusha so that she fell.

Dai Bando immediately reached down and lifted her to her feet.

"Thank you, Dai."

"You're welcome, Jerusha."

At the center of the arena, Jerusha saw seven stakes, with chains attached, set in the ground in a semicircle. She pondered them, then glanced quickly at the others. *We might not have much time in this world,* she thought, *but at least we can go to meet God with courage.*

A voice suddenly arose, carrying over the vast multitude that had gathered, and the prisoners turned toward a raised platform directly in front of the stakes. On it sat the Grand Wizards with Melchior and Iona in the center and seated slightly forward.

"It is not too late for you," Melchior said. He stood to his feet, and there was a cold smile on his lips. "If you would live, all you need do is renounce the One you serve—this Jesus. What say you?"

An unearthly quiet settled over the vast arena. Not a person stirred. Not a word was spoken.

Jerusha knew that this was the moment when they all must declare if they were really for Jesus Christ or were merely lip servants.

Mei-Lani looked at the wizards, sensing the evil that emanated from them. She reached back in her history and remembered stories of men and women and young people who had died in arenas such as this, some torn to pieces by wild beasts, some burned, some crucified. "I will never forsake You, Lord Jesus," she said, "and You will never forsake me."

Raina heard her and smiled. Her head was high, and there were courage and honor and dignity in her posture. Her eyes met those of Melchior steadily. She did not need to answer aloud. Her intent was plain.

Heck Jordan, next to her, was trembling. He knew that he was weak, but he had made his decision. Somehow he lifted his head and whispered, "No, I won't."

"God will be with you, Heck," Jerusha said. She lifted her head also, looking like a young Viking with her ash blonde hair and dark blue eyes. She stood tall and proud and said, "You may do what you will with your evil powers, but I will never forsake my God!"

"Nor will I," Dai Bando said quickly. Strong and able-looking, he put his arm around his aunt.

Bronwen smiled up at him, then said in a surprisingly strong voice, "None of us will recant. Do your worst!"

Ringo Smith had not yet spoken, but now he cried out, "You may kill the body, but the spirit will be preserved until the day of Christ Jesus."

At the words *Christ Jesus*, Melchior put his hands over his ears, as if an awful sound had pierced them. He uttered a wild cry, then screamed, "Chain them to the stakes! Prepare to execute!"

The guards shoved the victims forward.

But before they could make fast the chains, Bronwen Llewellen cried out, "It is time to see the hand of God! In the name of Jesus Christ, I rebuke you, you powers of darkness!"

Her words were like a fiery whip striking Melchior and Iona across the face. Both half turned away, and the lesser wizards became pale.

Iona recovered first. Pointing a long finger toward the prisoners, she began to shower them with curses.

161

Then, glancing around, she said, "Join me, you fools! They cannot stand against the power of our master!"

Immediately all the wizards were on their feet, calling upon Satan and the powers of darkness to destroy the captives. But what they said was not as fearsome as their twisted expressions. Evil seemed to shoot forth from their eyes.

"Be of good cheer," Bronwen said. "We have one weapon, and we must use it now."

"What is it, Aunt?" Dai asked. He was down on one knee. Physically he may have been the strongest man on the planet, but clearly he felt the dark pressure of evil. "What shall we do?"

Ringo gasped, "What *should* we do, Bronwen?"

"We must leave the outcome in the hands of our God, but He gave us the name above all names as our shield. Now, we must use it." Straightening, she lifted her voice above all other sounds in the arena.

"In the name of Jesus Christ of Nazareth, I stand against you powers of darkness. In the name of Jesus there is power . . ."

"That's it!" Mei-Lani cried. She also began to loudly praise Jesus Christ and the Father. Soon all of the prisoners were following Bronwen's example. Even Heck did his pitiful best to join in.

It was like war in the arena—not a war of swords or of Neuromags but of spiritual power flowing back and forth. At times the wizards seemed almost to overcome the small group that stood by the stakes. During those times, the skies darkened, thunder rolled ominously, and there were lightning flashes. Among the spectators, some fell to their knees. Others screamed and fled. Most stayed.

"We are the army of the living God," Bronwen

called, "and Jesus Christ is Lord of this planet. We call upon Him to bring utter victory."

Jerusha had fallen back against a stake, her breath taken by the immense evil that was like a wave crashing over her. Her mind reeled, but she called out, "Oh, Lord, help us! Defeat Your enemies, the powers of darkness!"

The others, too, began to pray in this way, and then it was that two of the wizards fell. Others cried out. Every time the name of Jesus was mentioned, they quivered. Melchior and the sorceress uttered curses as they witnessed power that they had not dreamed of.

"Executioner! Kill them! Kill them now!" Iona screamed.

The man dressed in black stepped forward with a short sword, and it was obvious that the spiritual battle was going to be ended by physical means.

But as the darksome creature advanced toward the victims, another cry rang out.

Jerusha turned to see, to her amazement, Temple Cole, hair in disarray and tears streaming down her cheeks.

"No! No!" the doctor cried, running straight to the executioner. "Mark! Help me! We must save them! We've been wrong!"

She threw herself on the man in black. Caught completely off guard, he fell headlong along with the doctor, who was trying her best to hold him.

Jerusha shot a glance at Captain Edge. His face was pale as milk. He seemed to be trying to break free from something. She saw, however, that the executioner was rising and was about to plunge his sword into Temple Cole.

"Dai, stop him!" she cried.

Dai sprang forward. His movement was almost quicker than the eye could follow. The executioner had time only to look once, and then Dai was upon him. A steely embrace closed about the dark-clad executioner's wrist, and he cried out in pain, dropping the sword. Dai said, "Be still! This is not your time!"

Captain Edge stood to the right of the wizards, watching with eyes full of misery and confusion and hopelessness.

Suddenly Raina ran to him. Putting both hands on his shoulders, she looked into his eyes and said, "Oh, Captain, it is time for you to come back." She shook him slightly, her fingers sinking into his shoulders. "In the name of Jesus," she said clearly, "I command you, powers of darkness, to leave this man alone! Jesus is Lord!"

At her last words, Mark uttered a cry and fell forward.

Raina cushioned his fall and then said, "Captain Edge! Captain Edge, look at me!"

Mark couldn't fully understand what was happening, but his head suddenly cleared, and he whispered, "Raina, I'm free."

Leaping to his feet, he looked at the wizards who had witnessed his rescue. He raised a hand and called out, "Your time of tyranny is over!"

Out in the crowd Mark saw Rowdan, Lanie, and other members of the resistance movement. But he knew now that physical resistance would not do. He called to one he had learned to trust.

"Bronwen?"

At once his navigator shouted in a voice like a trumpet, "All who believe in the Christ come and join against the powers of darkness."

It was a masterstroke. Hundreds of people surged forward.

Bronwen urged them on. "Come," she cried, "we will join together. Satan is defeated here this day."

Melchior and Iona, their eyes suddenly filled with fear, began to call on their masters to help them, but it was useless. More and more believers swept onto the field until the wizards were surrounded by a vast throng.

Iona, the sorceress, let out a meaningless cry and fell to the ground.

"Help her, someone," Bronwen called out.

"Help her?" Ringo stared. "They tried to kill us!"

"She is a troubled human being who needs our help," Bronwen said stoutly.

At that instant, Melchior began forcing his way into the crowd. His strength was such that he broke through, calling for his followers. But very few chose to join him.

When he had disappeared beyond the multitude, Mark Edge said, "Shall I go after him, Bronwen?"

"No, let the poor man go. Perhaps God in His mercy will find him one day."

Then Captain Edge's eyes met those of Rowdan. "I don't know much about this, Rowdan. I myself am not a believer." He looked around at his young friends, then at Bronwen, and his face was serious. "But I've seen something here that I never thought to see. I never would have thought that victory might be brought about without physical weapons."

"You have learned a valuable lesson, Captain," Rowdan said. He put an arm around his wife and raised his hand for silence. When all was quiet, he said, "It's time for the true men and women of Merlin to take possession of this planet. We will purge out the evil. The battle is not over yet. It is just begun. Are you with me?"

A mighty shout went up. The joy of victory could be seen on faces that had been filled with despair.

Ringo walked over to Raina and said, "I guess we won."

"It's the Lord who's won," she said simply. "You know we could never have done it."

"That's right." Ringo took a deep breath. "And it's good to be on the winning side for once."

Mark Edge was still trying to put it all together. And then, suddenly, he remembered something.

He found Temple Cole standing well back in the crowd. Her head was bowed, and her shoulders were shaking. He put a hand under her chin and lifted her head, looking into her tear-stained face. "What happened to you, Temple?"

The doctor said, "I don't know, Mark. All I know is that I went wrong somewhere. I've hurt you terribly, and the Rangers too. I tried to betray you all. You must hate me dreadfully."

Mark shook his head. "I don't do any such thing." He saw that the ensigns had followed him. "Look, Temple. What do you see?"

Temple Cole blinked and brushed the tears from her cheeks. She looked from face to face, and on every face was a smile. Beginning with Mei-Lani, she heard them one by one say words of love and forgiveness. When all had spoken, she began to tremble. "I don't know if I can ever be clean again. What I did was so awful!"

Raina, Mei-Lani, and Jerusha glanced at one another. They seemed to have agreed on something. They quickly surrounded the surgeon, and Raina St.

Clair said, "We're going to be great friends, Dr. Cole. And there *is* a way to be clean. We'll tell you about it."

And then Temple Cole looked up, met the eyes of Captain Edge, and seemed to find something there that pleased her. "Is it all right, Mark?"

"It's all right, Temple. You're still our chief surgeon." He looked around. "I guess we old folks have something to learn from these who are younger."

Watching, Bronwen Llewellen smiled. "Wisdom is where you find it, in young or old, Captain. I know *this* is a day you will never forget!"

16

No Place Like Earth

The *Daystar* sat in an open field, surrounded by thousands of cheering people. It looked as though most of Merlina had turned out to bid the crew farewell. The crew members stood at attention before the new rulers of the planet, Rowdan and Lanie. There had been many speeches, and now Rowdan raised his hand for silence.

"You have been brought to this place by the hand of our God," he said simply. His voice carried over the vast space clearly, and he spoke for some time about how God had answered prayers that had been prayed for years. Then he said, "You have fought a spiritual battle, and now the victory is the Lord's."

Rousing cries went up. For a time the new ruler and his wife could only wait.

Mark Edge stood in front of his crew, who were lined up in military formation. He studied the faces of the young ones and, not for the first time, wondered how youth could make such an impact on a mission.

Temple Cole stood beside him, and she seemed to read his thoughts. "They are a phenomenal group of young people."

"They are. And I still don't understand it all."

Then the ceremony was over, all the good-byes were said, and they entered the star cruiser. Captain Edge took his stand on the bridge. "Prepare to exit!"

He moved the thruster controls, and *Daystar* rose smoothly into the air. Edge hovered over the city for a

169

few minutes, then pointed the nose of the ship straight up. *Daystar's* powerful engines rocketed the cruiser through the Merlinian atmosphere. Breaking the sound barrier, the spaceship caused a thunderous boom to echo through the city.

As they moved out and the planet Merlina became smaller and smaller, Edge said to Zeno Thrax, "A successful mission, First."

"I feel like I was out of most of it, but everything turned out well. I wish I could have been there and seen the defeat of the wizards."

Edge did not answer for a time. Then he looked at Zeno and said, "What do you think about all of this?"

"You mean about the Christians?"

"Yes."

"I think any reasonable man would have to say there is something to it, Captain. Don't you agree?"

Captain Edge nodded shortly. "It appears that there is something to it."

Zeno's lips curled upward in a smile. "The doctor has changed. Did you know that I can understand how she thinks quite easily now?"

"What is she thinking?"

Thrax suddenly grew aloof. "I would never reveal such a thing as that! It would not be ethical!" But he smiled. "For instance, would you like for me to reveal to the doctor what *you* are thinking right now?"

Edge whirled and walked off, saying, "You have the bridge, Mr. Thrax!"

He walked through the ship, speaking to the crew hardly at all. He was preoccupied and wanted to get away to his cabin to think about what had happened. When he stepped inside, he heard a slight noise and pivoted quickly, his hands in a defensive position. And then he dropped them.

"Temple!" he exclaimed. "What are you doing here?"

Dr. Cole did not speak for a moment, and then she whispered, "Mark, I still can't seem to find my way out. I feel so awful!"

Edge moved closer. His voice was gentle as he said, "Temple, you don't have to apologize every time we meet. You have already apologized. You have been forgiven. You made a mistake—but so did I. We all make them."

"Can you really forgive me?"

"Of course! Everyone already has. You're just going to have to learn to accept that and forgive yourself."

"Thank you, Mark." The doctor suddenly smiled shyly and looked up. "You're a generous man."

"Never been called that."

"You are, though. You must spend a great deal of time perfecting this tough guy image that you're so proud of. But underneath it you're not all that tough. You know what Thrax says about you?"

"I don't care what Thrax says."

"He says you're a marshmallow inside."

"Oh, he does! Well, we'll see about that! Maybe some extra work will convince him—"

Temple reached up and put her fingers on his lips. "Don't be angry. I feel the same way."

When she removed her hand and started to leave, Mark took her by the arm and turned her around. He cleared his throat and said, "I've always been a tough sort of fellow, rough and not much polish. You can see that."

"Well, that's been your boast. I can't say as I've seen much of it."

Then he said, "I see it's going to take me a long time to convince you what a varmint I really am."

"Oh, really? Then I think you'd better begin."

They left the cabin, and before they had reached the lounge area, both were laughing.

Mei-Lani watched Jerusha during their journey back to Earth. Finally she could stand it no longer. She went to her friend and said, "Jerusha, I know you were really sweet on Captain Edge."

"No, I wasn't," Jerusha said, but her face reddened.

"A wise man once said, 'Know thyself.' You know so much about other people. Surely you can see this about yourself."

Jerusha suddenly laughed. "Everybody's tried to tell me this. But, really, I just admire the captain, that's all."

Mei-Lani looked at the beautiful girl before her and knew that this was not the full truth. However, she said only, "I'm your friend, Jerusha."

"Well, I know that." Jerusha changed the subject abruptly, saying, "It's going to be quite a banquet tonight. We should go help with it."

"All right. I've got some wonderful dishes planned."

"You know the captain doesn't like strange things. You don't have any of those, do you?"

"Nothing but eyeball soup."

"Eyeball soup!"

"I was just kidding. Let's get started."

Edge had put on the brand-new uniform that he had saved for a special occasion. It was dark green with gold trim at the neck and on the cuffs. It fit tightly and showed off his athletic figure to perfection. He studied himself in the mirror and brushed his hair carefully.

"Hey, now, you look pretty good for an old man!" he told his reflection.

He found that the rec room had been turned into a banquet hall. The ensigns had decorated it with spangles and colored streamers and a display of revolving lights. He blinked at the sight.

Everyone rose when he came in, and he found himself speechless. "Well, I didn't realize that I was such an important person." He approached the dessert table, checking out the bowls of gelatin and all sorts of pies and cakes. He saw that they were his favorites. Leaning over the table, he said, "I wonder if I could possibly have some of all—"

Suddenly a blow struck him from behind. He knew instantly what it was, but he could not help himself. He went crashing into the table, bringing it down, as an ocean of desserts splashed onto his face, hair, and uniform. He rolled over, shouting, "Jerusha! Get this animal out of here before I kill her!"

Jerusha pulled Contessa back, scolding her, and sent her away with her tail between her legs. Then she knelt down beside him. "Oh, Captain, I'm so sorry." She dabbed at his face with a napkin, then tried to get the orange marmalade gelatin out of his hair. "I'm so sorry," she repeated.

"You did that on purpose! You trained that dog to do that!" Edge shouted.

"Really I haven't, Captain. It's just that—she just loves you so much."

The others had gathered around, not daring to laugh, although Edge presumed that he made a ridiculous figure sitting there with orange marmalade gelatin in his hair, strawberry gelatin on his face and chest, and chocolate mousse all the way down his pants to his boots.

Zeno Thrax shook his head in disapproval. "You shouldn't even think thoughts like that, Captain!" he muttered.

Edge got to his feet and looked down at himself. "What a mess," he groaned.

"I'll wash your uniform. It'll be prettier than ever, Captain," Jerusha said.

"Why does that dog have to love *me?*"

Jerusha winked at the others. "You're just so lovable, Captain, that no female can resist you."

At this a laugh did go up. Even Zeno Thrax doubled over.

Ivan Petroski had a deep, booming laugh for such a small person. His eyes twinkled merrily. "I think that's true, Captain. You might as well learn to live with it."

Suddenly Edge began to smile. Then he laughed out loud.

"All right. Go on and laugh, all of you—but you'll be sorry! Just wait until the next mission! I'm going to make you wish you'd never been born." He looked over at Temple, who was still trying to keep a straight face, and said, "Now, you're going to see what a mean and unpleasant fellow I really am. Totally heartless!"

Temple Cole fought down a smile. "Pay attention to Captain Edge," she said. "He's the meanest man in the galaxy. He admits it freely." Then she said, "I do think we must have a toast."

They all scrambled to find punch glasses of some sort, and soon everyone had something in his hand.

The doctor raised her glass and said, "Here's to

Captain Mark Edge, captain of the *Daystar* and the best captain in the galaxy—despite his meanness."

All began to cry out, "Hear! Hear!"

Then Mark filled his glass and raised it. And no one appeared to consider him ridiculous-looking, even though smeared with dessert from head to foot. "And here's to the Junior Space Rangers of the *Daystar.*" He hesitated, then a fond expression came over his face. "To the Rangers. May they always be what they are now—the finest crew I've ever seen."

As the *Daystar* swept through endless space, outside it was cold, but inside was warmth and joy.

Ringo Smith felt complete for the first time in his life. "It's great, isn't it, Heck!" he exclaimed.

Heck Jordan winked. "Wait till you hear my plan!" he announced. His eyes gleamed, and he began to talk excitedly until he saw that Ringo was not listening but had his eyes fixed on Raina St. Clair.

"I get no respect!" Heck grumbled—then began to speak loudly about how on the *next* mission to Makon, they would all become rich and famous.

Get swept away in the many Gilbert Morris Adventures

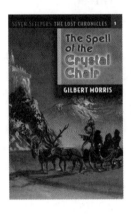

The Lost Chronicles

Tales of the popular Seven Sleepers are discovered! The adventures get more exciting as the Sleepers follow Goel in their battle against the forces of darkness.
Growing series for ages 7-12.

Daystar Voyages

Join the crew of the Daystar as they traverse the wide expanse of space. Adventure and danger abound, but they learn time and again that God is truly the Master of the Universe.
Ten Book Series for ages 7-12.

The Seven Sleepers

Go with Josh and his friends as they are sent by Goel, their spiritual leader, on dangerous and challenging voyages to conquer the forces of darkness in the new world. Ten book Series for ages 10-14